LAWLESS &
TILLEY

Magic Eye

MALCOLM ROSE

■SCHOLASTIC

Have you read?

Lawless & Tilley 1: The Secrets of the Dead
Lawless & Tilley 2: Deep Waters

Look out for:

Lawless & Tilley 4: Still Life

For Brian, Joan and Hugh

Scholastic Children's Books
Commonwealth House, 1–19 New Oxford Street,
London WC1A 1NU, UK
a division of Scholastic Ltd
London ~ New York ~ Toronto ~ Sydney ~ Auckland

First published in the UK by Scholastic Ltd, 1998

Copyright © Malcolm Rose, 1998

Map copyright © Bartholomew 1997. Reproduced with
permission of HarperCollins Cartographic. MM-0997-26
"Song in the Blood" is taken from *Paroles* by Jacques Prévert,
© Editions Gallimard, 1949. The English translation is by
Lawrence Ferlinghetti, © Ferlinghetti, 1958.

ISBN 0 590 13934 7

Typeset by TW Typesetting, Midsomer Norton, Somerset
Printed by Cox & Wyman Ltd, Reading, Berks.

10 9 8 7 6 5 4 3 2 1

All rights reserved

The right of Malcolm Rose to be identified as the author
of this work has been asserted by him in accordance with the
Copyright, Designs and Patents Act, 1988.

This book is sold subject to the condition that it shall not,
by way of trade or otherwise, be lent, resold, hired out, or
otherwise circulated without the publisher's prior consent
in any form of binding or cover other than that in which it
is published and without a similar condition, including this
condition, being imposed upon the subsequent purchaser.

1

Nicola Morrison died because she didn't have the strength to loosen the last nut on the front nearside wheel of her Peugeot. Her car, lamed by a puncture, was parked on the kerb of the A57 and her body lay not far away, by the bushes that bounded the eighth green of a nearby golf course. She was a slight young woman, nineteen years of age, with beautifully groomed long brown hair. She'd been very pretty until her skull had been shattered with the wheelbrace, like an eggshell cracked with a spoon. If the killer had tried to hide her corpse, the attempt had been half-hearted at best. Maybe he wanted her to be found, or perhaps he'd been disturbed before finishing the job of concealing her body under the shrub.

To Detective Inspector Brett Lawless of the South Yorkshire Police, it looked obvious. Next to the flat tyre beside the car, there was a jack, the wheelbrace, spare tyre and watery bloodstains. Three of the wheel nuts were loose. The other was still firmly fixed in place. Nicola had been driving along the A57 when her car had suffered a puncture. From the boot, she'd extracted the jack, spare tyre and wheelbrace. She'd tried to loosen all of the wheel nuts before jacking up the car, removing the nuts, and replacing the flat with the spare. Three of the four nuts had yielded to her efforts but the fourth had been obstinate. It had refused to budge. Nicola must have breathed a sigh of relief when some big-hearted, big-muscled man stopped to lend a hand.

Her relief would have been short-lived. The Good Samaritan had not come to her rescue. He'd come to kill. He'd grabbed the wheelbrace and, instead of tackling the final wheel nut, he'd attacked her. He'd dropped the weapon by the car and dragged her body down on to the golf course, leaving a trail of blood. Afterwards, he must have walked back to the road and driven away in his own vehicle. During the day the A57 was a busy road so Brett anticipated that Nicola had been murdered last night in the dark. In his mind, he could almost see the dreadful crime being acted out. The motive was much less clear. Brett could not see into the brain of the murderer.

Nicola's body was fully clothed and the pathologist informed Brett that there were no signs of assault, other than the head wound. The leader of the forensic team reported that the victim's purse contained two visa cards and several banknotes, the radio cassette player had not been wrenched from her car, and the key was still in the ignition. Plainly, the killer was not interested in robbery or joyriding. The forensic scientist believed that the scene had remained undisturbed until a curious and observant commuter, puzzled by the crippled car, had stopped in the early morning and used her mobile phone to call the police.

Most puzzling of all, the murderer had left a message in his victim's coat pocket. It was a piece of yellow card with words cut out from newspaper headlines glued on to it. Somehow the different sizes and styles of the words made the message even more mysterious, cold and threatening.

You will *be* getting to **know** me

As if the discarded body weren't enough evidence, the calling card confirmed it. The killer's calculating, inhuman brain was twisted beyond repair. Brett shivered. The implications of the message haunted him.

The golf course was west of Worksop, near Woodsetts, on the main road into Sheffield. At the southern boundary of the course, there was a wooded hill. Behind it ran the railway and the disused Chesterfield canal. A tent now marked the spot by the eighth hole where Nicola's body had been dumped. From her car to the green, the area was separated from the rational world by a ring of police ribbon. On the road, uniformed officers were waving the traffic past the spectacle, discouraging morbid sightseers who threatened to clog the A57 completely.

Surveying the scene of the crime, Brett cursed his luck. Until last night, January had brought Siberia to South Yorkshire but overnight the winds had turned, bringing in much warmer weather. A rapid thaw had set in. Now, on Wednesday 17th January, neither the turf of the golf course nor the grass verge retained enough ice and snow to preserve a frozen memory of footprints or tyre tracks. It was still chilly but not chilly enough to solidify the evidence of shoes or a car. If someone had raised the alarm last night, the forensic scientists could have read the imprint of the crime in the snow. By morning, though, the record had been erased, melted away. Now, the members of the forensic crew, dressed in white overalls, were padding about on a soggy and slippery surface.

It was three o'clock in the afternoon. The scene-of-crime team had been working non-stop since early morning. They had finished their grim trawl for clues in the immediate vicinity and the pathologist had made his initial deductions. Before he removed the body for further examination back in the morgue, Brett asked him, "What's your best time of death?"

"I can't be exact," he replied. "When I first got here this morning – seven-thirty – she felt more or less cold and stiff. Eight hours, possibly, as a crude estimate. Under her clothes, hypostasis suggests she was left on her back when she was killed and hasn't been disturbed since. For the post-mortem interval I normally rely on inner body temperature, but it isn't very helpful here because the rate of cooling will have changed a lot overnight. You see, she was murdered last night at a low temperature and then her body was exposed to steadily increasing temperatures throughout the night. Difficult to correct for. Let's say she weighs in at fifty kilograms. And she's got at least three layers of clothing insulating her, but they were all cold and damp. And she was exposed to a considerable wind." He shrugged. "When I do the calculation, assume she was at thirty-seven Celsius when she died and plug in her temperature at seven-fifty this morning, I bet it'll come out at a post-mortem interval of six to ten hours. I won't be able to pin it down more precisely than that. Too many variables."

"Thanks," Brett said. "But basically she was killed between about ten o'clock last night and two in the morning," he concluded.

The pathologist nodded. "Yes. Single blow to the head. Not a frenzied attack, just one very hard blow. No messing. Cause of death: cranial damage."

"Will her attacker have got blood on his clothing – assuming it was a he?"

"I should think so. The scalp is very vascular. It would've bled profusely. And it would've carried on bleeding after death, so his coat and hands – or gloves – would almost certainly have got blood-stained. If he didn't get covered ~~in blood~~, it'd be down to pure luck. Last night there'd have been a lot more blood around here as well, but most of it's soaked away with the melt water."

When Brett asked to speak to the officers who had arrived on the scene first, two Nottinghamshire constables from Worksop were brought to him. One was a youngster, barely past her GCSEs, and the other was in his fifties. On his broad shoulders there were specks of dandruff like tiny snowflakes that had not yet melted. No doubt the experienced officer had taken the new recruit under his wing. First, Brett asked the older constable, "What's your name?"

The constable could not keep a smug grin from his face. "Law, sir," he stated, waiting for Brett to make a joke that the policeman had heard regularly over his thirty years in the force. When Brett didn't rise to the bait, the uniformed officer added, "With a name like that, I just had to end up in the police force."

"Mmm." After seeing the victim and reading the calling card, Brett was not really in the mood for banter. And he had enough trouble with his own name. Even so, he didn't want to appear humourless so he replied, "I don't know what that says for me, then: Brett Lawless." He turned to the novice and queried, "What about you? Not Constable Copps or something like that?"

The policewoman tried to smile. "No. Louise

Jenson." She looked upset.

"Is this your first call-out?" Brett asked.

"No, sir. But it's my first—"

"Murder? Never easy," Brett said sympathetically. "But I hope you never see enough of it to lose the sense of shock." He said it as a man who, at the age of twenty-seven, had already seen too much death. Talking to her partner again, Brett asked, "You spoke to the woman who found the car?"

The constable answered, "Yes. Anna Stimpson." From his notebook, he read out her home address and her place of work. She was the director of a theatrical agency in Sheffield. "She saw the car and some bloodstains, she said, and then she called us. Five past seven this morning. She was told to wait here till we arrived and could take her statement and details. She didn't see the body, apparently. We," he said, glancing at his new colleague, "discovered the body."

Brett commented, "You're out of your area."

"Yes. Apparently, the caller said the incident was close to Worksop so it came to us, not realizing it was actually in South Yorkshire. We alerted your force but stayed on till you arrived to provide assistance."

"Thanks." To make Louise feel useful, Brett asked her, "And what did you make of her, this Anna Stimpson?"

Somewhat nervously, she replied, "A big woman. Well dressed. No wedding ring. Probably career-minded. Drove a new BMW. She pulled on to the verge just beyond the victim's car," she said, pointing to the spot.

"Do you think she was telling the truth when she said she didn't see the body?"

Louise paused before answering, "Yes, I think so."

"What about you?" he asked Constable Law.

The old hand shrugged. "I've got no reason to suspect she was lying, but I was more interested in getting down her details because I knew you detectives would want to check her out for yourselves." He said it spitefully, as if he expected Brett to regard his opinion as worthless. Over the years, he'd probably been put down too many times by cocky superiors.

"OK," Brett responded. "Thanks." Before he left them, he added, "You did well. You can head back over the border now."

"Facts," Brett announced. "That's what we need right now, and lots of them." It was early evening and Brett had called together his team – minus one of its most important members. "Let's think about how we're going to get them. What are the angles? Passers-by who saw Nicola's Peugeot last night. Even better, we need to trace anyone who saw *two* cars stopped by the golf course. How about members of the golf club?"

"Golf isn't one of your games, is it, Boss?" Greg called out. "Not many play golf at midnight, you know. Especially when the holes are stuffed full of snow and ice."

Brett grinned. He could cope with Detective Sergeant Greg Lenton's cheek because it was good-natured. It hadn't always been. When Brett was promoted to probationary detective inspector above Greg, there had been real animosity, but that was before Greg had witnessed Brett's knack for solving tricky cases. Now the jokes weren't delivered to wound. "No," Brett responded, "golf isn't my strong point, but a birdie tells me that enthusiasts might still go to the clubhouse. And they might just be leaving at the time when Nicola was killed. The clubhouse is at the end of a short lane on the Worksop side of the course." He pointed to the map that had already been pinned to a wall. "The road's a dead end. Just serves a farm and the clubhouse, according to the map. We need to check the members who were there last night. Other angles? We need someone to trace Nicola's movements. Was she being followed by our man or did he just take advantage of a roadside breakdown? We also need to know all about Nicola. What sort of person was she? Friends, relatives, boyfriends, ex-boyfriends – anything. Once we get some facts, we might start to see some sense in all this."

Brett paused before adding, "The media. We might need to put out a call through the media for information from the public, but not just yet. First, tonight – ten till two – there's a chance we can stir someone's memory. Know what I've got in mind, Greg?"

"You're going to put me in charge of a road block," Greg groaned. "It's a well-used road. We stop traffic tonight and ask any drivers who trundle along it regularly what they saw last night. You want facts – and sightings."

"Exactly. Use as many officers as you think you need, Greg." Looking round the incident room, Brett said, "Mark and Paula – you broke the news to Nicola's family, didn't you? OK, well, I want you to go back and do some gentle probing about friends, what she got up to, where she went last night and who she went with, whatever you can find out. The rest of you are on routine inquiries at the farm and clubhouse. I'm going to speak to Anna Stimpson – the woman who discovered Nicola's car."

Brett took a deep breath and finished his briefing by saying, "You all know about the calling card. We keep it to ourselves for the moment. OK, everyone? But I don't need to tell you what it might mean. *You'll be getting to know me.* He might be planning another strike right now. He might be sticking more words on a card. I don't think we want to let him get much further, so it's important we pull out all the stops on this one. Now, I've called our killer 'he' because men make more likely roadside rescuers and they're much more likely to commit murder than women. But let's not be blind to *any* possibility at this stage.

"Tomorrow," Brett concluded, "you'll be pleased to know we'll be joined by Clare – if she's well enough – and she'll partner me. We'll want to follow up any leads, particularly Nicola's mates and boy-friend, if there is one, and drivers or golfers who saw something or think they may have seen something but they're not sure it's worth reporting. So, names, addresses and telephone numbers of any hopefuls, please. The forensic evidence will start to roll in as well. I want all of it to come to me. Reports straight into my folder in a computer. Once you've had those diplomatic words with the Morrison family, Mark, can you set up a computer system? You did a good job on the Upper Needless case."

"That was when I had help from Liz," Mark admitted. "She's the real power behind the computer. She's the techno-junkie."

Brett smiled. "I know. I'll see what I can do. As soon as I think I can justify it, I'll try and get the Chief to assign her to this case. For the moment, you sort it out. All right?"

Anna Stimpson was a formidable woman. Middle-aged and perhaps five feet ten. If Clare had been beside her, Anna would have been slightly shorter but she would have weighed considerably more. She was not plump, but muscular. She had dark starchy hair, worn short like a man's, and she was dressed in smart starchy clothes even though she was relaxing at home with a gin and tonic. Her portable computer, diary and mobile phone, now lying on the coffee table, probably never left her side. On the same table, there was a magazine with a picture of a dog on the cover as well as copies of *The Times*, the *Daily Telegraph* and the *Guardian*.

Brett wanted to interview her not because he was suspicious of her but because of what he had been taught. The calling card suggested that the person who had murdered Nicola was a potential serial killer. Brett's former boss, Big John Macfarlane, now promoted to Detective Chief Superintendent of North Wales Police, had once said to him, "Some killers do report finding their victims. They think it deflects suspicion. Serial killers in particular have been known to inject themselves into the investigation of their murders. They appear to be helpful to the case but really they're making it a game between themselves and us." Brett wanted to see Anna Stimpson for himself. He wanted to try and guess if she was playing deadly games. He would have been happier if Clare had been with him rather than tucked up in bed with flu. Brett was a facts-and-theory fiend whereas Clare was more a people person. That was why they made a good partnership.

"So," Brett asked, "you were driving into your office this morning—"

"Seven o'clock," she said, interrupting as if she hadn't got the patience to wait for Brett to reach the end of his question.

"What made you stop?"

"I wasn't going to – I didn't have a lot of time – but it seemed all wrong. I could see the flat tyre. No one abandons a car just because they've got a flat. You see, I drive around a lot on my own. I can understand the vulnerability of lone drivers, especially if they're female."

Anna was hardly the vulnerable type, Brett mused,

but he accepted that she might have been concerned. "And you found…?"

"Unlocked car, key in the ignition and what looked like blood on the ground. I called the police."

"Did you see anything else? A body?"

"No," Anna stated. "I'd seen enough to worry me without looking any further." At her feet sat two alert Dobermann pinschers, their short black and tan coats impressively shiny.

"Did you touch anything? The car, the jack or spare tyre?"

"No. Nothing. The whole thing gave me the creeps. I left it well alone." For a woman, her voice was low and husky.

"Do you take the same route home?" Brett queried. "Along the A57?"

"Yes."

"What time did you get home last night? Did you see the same Peugeot then?"

"No," Anna answered. "I hadn't seen it before. And I got home about six-thirty last night. A bit earlier than normal but the road conditions were so atrocious, I set out early."

"You didn't go out on the same road later last night, did you?"

"No. I stayed in. I like to read the newspapers and reviews in the evening."

Realizing that Brett did not pose a physical threat to his owner, one of the Dobermanns lay down, stretched out and issued a sleepy sigh.

"Did you know the victim?" Brett asked, deliberately not providing any information.

"I don't know. Was she from round here?"

"I didn't say the victim was a woman."

Anna grimaced. "They did on local radio as I drove home. They didn't give her name, though. They just reported that she was a young woman." Anna shook her head. "Terrible. She was battered to death, wasn't she?"

"Is that what you heard on the radio news?" Brett responded warily.

"No. It comes from having seen one of those heavy car spanners with blood on it. An extremely unpleasant and distressing sight, I might add. Unfortunately, one's imagination fills in the gaps."

Suddenly, Brett felt cold and queasy as if he were starved of oxygen. For a second, he didn't understand what was happening to him. He felt scared and uncertain. Anna's comment had dredged up a buried memory from somewhere in his subconscious. As soon as it surfaced, it disappeared again mysteriously before he could grasp it, understand it. He wasn't even sure that he would have had the will to hang on to the image because it was so powerful and terrifying. He let it go on purpose. It was best left safely submerged – or suppressed.

"Are you all right?" Anna enquired.

"Er … yes. Thanks. Murder *is* distressing, I'm afraid." Still unsettled, but slowly recovering from his own fleeting shock, he said, "The victim's called

Nicola. Do you know a teenager called Nicola who drives a Peugeot?"

Anna breathed heavily. "No, definitely not. But I feel for her – and her family."

Brett left with few answers. He had not learned much about Anna Stimpson – he could not yet rule her out of the inquiry – but he realized that he might be on the verge of learning a lot about himself. Painful things that he'd rather not know.

Beguiled, Brett gazed at the Magic Eye picture pinned to his fridge door with a magnetic clamp. While he drank cold fruit juice, he frowned at the apparently meaningless shapes and symbols. He knew that he was supposed to be able to conjure a coherent hidden image from the tangled pattern but his eyes refused to see it. He viewed it from close up and then took a few steps backward to peer at it from a distance. It didn't help. Either way, the true picture eluded him. He shook his head. His partner, Detective Sergeant Clare Tilley, had given him the Magic Eye poster for Christmas and he could only assume that it was part of a diabolical plot to drive him insane. He was haunted by his inability to summon an image from the pattern.

Two peeps from a car horn heralded Clare's

arrival. Brett grabbed his coat and put it on while he headed for the front door. As soon as he slipped into the car, he looked sympathetically at his partner and asked, "How are you feeling? You look…" He hesitated, not finding an apt but diplomatic adjective to describe her. Her nose was raw and sore, almost as red as her hair. The rest of her face was whiter than normal and her skin's natural sheen had been dulled by the infection.

Clare waited, daring Brett to voice his verdict. She still blamed him for her illness because, at the end of their last case, he had sprayed her with freezing cold water. In ribbing him about the repercussions, it suited her to ignore the fact that he'd saved her from being sprayed with acid instead.

"You look like you're coping with it better than I would," Brett said generously.

"Well," Clare retorted, "if you catch it from me, we'll find out!"

Brett laughed. "Giving a virus to your superior officer counts as mutiny. It warrants a severe reprimand."

Clare coughed and then replied, "You don't know the rules well enough. It doesn't count at all with a *probationary* superior. Anyway," she said before Brett could respond, "where are we going? HQ?"

"Yes. Via a golf course near Worksop."

"Worksop? That's Notts Constabulary land."

"The body was on our side of the border so we're dealing with it – with cooperation from the Worksop crew. Anyway," Brett explained, "I want you to get a sniff of the scene of the crime first."

Clare groaned. "Don't talk to me about sniffing!"

Brett laughed again. "On the way there, I'll tell you what we know."

The eighth green was still under curfew, guarded by two uniformed officers, encircled by blue and white ribbon and a posse of press photographers. Brett and Clare ducked under the ribbon. The white tent was still in place, like a large bubble, but Nicola's body had been taken away. Outside, two forensic scientists were still conducting their intricate analysis of the surrounding patch of ground, looking for fibres and any other foreign matter.

"So this is where she was dumped," Clare remarked hoarsely, "complete with calling card."

"*You'll be getting to know me*," Brett repeated glumly. "Do you get the feeling that this is just the start – that there are more messages to come?"

Clare nodded ruefully. "Afraid so. Or maybe it's not his first. See what I mean? *You'll be getting to know me*. It could mean he's killed before and we haven't realized it yet."

Brett nodded slowly. "Good point. Flu does wonders for you. We need to follow that up, and I know the best person for it."

Clare smiled. "Liz!"

"There's no one better at digging around in databases, finding links. When we get back, I'll go and see the boss. I might have enough of a case to persuade him to release her for the job."

"Good idea," Clare said. "You know something else about this calling-card business? It means last night he set out with murder in mind. To be carrying his charming little message, he must have made a conscious decision to go out, cruising around looking for a victim. I bet Nicola was chosen at random. She died because she was available, courtesy of a flat tyre."

"Forensics are checking it was a real puncture, rather than someone letting her tyre down on purpose."

Clare breathed in deeply. "You know," she added with a frown, "it's the image I have of him, sitting at home, cutting letters and words out of newspapers, that bothers me. It's so deliberate. So premeditated. There's some warped reasoning going on inside his skull."

Brett agreed. "I wonder how many calling cards he's made and what they say."

Last night's trawl had netted four drivers. Two leaving the clubhouse had seen the stranded Peugeot and two other late-night travellers remembered noticing Nicola's parked car. The earliest sighting was twelve-twenty and the latest was roughly one-fifteen. None of the four had seen a second vehicle parked near Nicola's car. Mark and Paula had discovered that Nicola had gone to a club that evening with her boyfriend, Lance Golby.

"We've got some interviewing to do," Brett announced.

"Yes," Clare replied. "I can understand us needing to see Lance Golby, but do we really need to speak to the motorists who've probably already told their all?"

"We do, yes," Brett decided. "Our man might be trying to get involved in the investigation. It might be a game to him – or her, I suppose. I think we need to take a quick look at all the witnesses, just in case. Any one of them might be trying to wheedle a way in. If he wants to make himself known to us, let's help him all we can."

"Fair enough," Clare said in a voice that had dropped an octave because of her cold. "We look for an unnatural curiosity in the murder or the progress of the investigation, then?"

"That's right. And you're the right person to do it. First, though," Brett said, "let's go and get updates from pathology and forensics. Then I try to convince the Chief we need Liz. After that, we do the grand tour of witnesses."

"I've got some bad news for you," the Chief Pathologist muttered as soon as he saw Brett. Tony Rudd had taken on Nicola's case. He always liked to put himself in charge of the interesting ones. "I haven't got any more on the cause of death – that's straightforward. And the fingernails show she didn't put up a fight – no one else's blood or skin or clothing behind them. Taken by surprise, it seems. But there *is* something you should know. I'm pretty sure a lock of hair's been snipped off. The victim had a lot of it, but there's definitely a shorter clump in there. An accident at the hairdresser's, perhaps, but it's also the typical profile of a serial killer. Hair's often taken as a memento of murder. Your man's starting a collection of keepsakes, I'm afraid. It won't be long before you get another body."

In the forensic laboratory, Greta informed Brett that the flat tyre was a result of a large nail. "The entry hole is consistent with it piercing the tyre when it was revolving rapidly. This wasn't done deliberately on a stationary tyre."

"What about the calling card?"

"We haven't got a source for the card itself but it's not remarkable in any way," Greta announced. "We've analysed the paper and ink and taken a good look at the fonts used in the message. The words came from two newspapers – the *Telegraph* and *The Times*. You've got a well read, high-class killer. The glue was one of those solvent-free glue sticks. We haven't pinned it down to a particular brand yet."

"OK," Brett said. "What about prints?"

"None on the card, I'm afraid – just the odd smear. It's clean. We've got dabs all over the car, though. Mostly the victim's, plus one other. Here's the big one: we found a second set of dabs on the wheelbrace. Someone other than the victim handled it. They didn't match anyone on our database."

"We'll work on that," Brett murmured. "Did the body turn up anything?"

"Not a lot. Alcohol in the blood, but she was under the legal limit. No funny substances. She wasn't a smoker but she'd been in a smoky atmosphere, judging by residue analysis on her clothing. Nothing to help you," Greta concluded with a shrug.

Detective Chief Superintendent Keith Johnstone listened to half of Brett's request and then interrupted. "What you're saying is, you want Liz because of something you're predicting might happen in the future. I can't run this section on intuition, you know. If it happens, I'll consider it then."

"It's not just that we might have a serial killer on our hands in the future," Brett persisted. "He might be one already. If he *has* killed before, there'll be more evidence available. We can make headway much quicker if Liz checks it out." Brett had learned that the arguments Keith liked best were based on speedier convictions. After all, he had his crime statistics and performance indicators to consider.

"All right, Brett. I suppose you haven't let me down yet. You can have Liz. I'll get her to report to you tomorrow morning."

"Thank you, sir."

Just as Brett was about to leave, the Chief said, "But there's something you've got to do in return. You're neglecting one aspect of this case – public relations. You're in charge now, Brett. No one else

23

takes care of it for you. Have you seen the local news? Press speculation is running wild. You need to hold a press conference."

Brett grimaced. "I haven't done one of those before."

"No time like the present," Keith rejoined. "Besides, everyone's got a secret desire to be on telly. I've got every confidence in you. There's only two rules: go in knowing exactly what you want to say and exactly what you need to keep a lid on. Never be badgered into revealing what you've decided to keep secret. Secondly, if you're after information from the public, try to find a relative of the victim who'll come over well on screen to make the appeal. That's all there is to it. The public relations officer will set it up for you. All you have to do is turn up and perform."

On the way to Lance Golby's house, Clare enquired, "You're not going to mention the calling card or lock of hair to the press, are you?"

"Definitely not," Brett confirmed. "Or the weapon."

"Just call it a blunt instrument," Clare suggested with a smile. "It's the phrase they use on all the best TV cop shows."

"Thanks for the advice," Brett replied sarcastically. "Really, we'll need to keep quiet about the wheelbrace, hair and the calling card so we can tell the difference between a true confession and any false ones later. We know about the message and so does the killer, but no one else does. It's useful to keep his trademarks to ourselves."

At a red light, Clare took the opportunity to swallow a couple of aspirin tablets in an attempt to lower her temperature and keep the aches and pains at bay. "I think you learned a lot from John Macfarlane in your first case," she ventured. "He always loathed talking to the press."

"Quite right," Brett said. "Big event for me. I'm not looking forward to it." He glanced at Clare and, to lighten the mood, added impishly, "It's not to be sneezed at, is it?"

In reply, Clare gave him a withering look.

Lance Golby was twenty-four years old, he lived with his parents and he worked as a freelance software engineer.

"Do you get plenty of jobs?" Clare asked to break the ice. "Computers seem to be everywhere. It can't be a bad business to be in."

"No," he agreed. Uninterestedly, he explained, "I programme computers for people, fix software problems, advise them. Make sure they get the best out of their information systems."

"I'm sorry about Nicola," Clare said softly, suppressing a sneeze. "How long had you been going out with her?"

Lance sighed heavily. "We'd been seeing each other, on and off, for a few months. We weren't... But we might've been."

"You mean, it might have got serious between you?"

He nodded sadly.

"Where did you go with her on Tuesday night?" Clare prompted.

"We just went to Mixers nightclub in Worksop."

"When did you leave?"

"When? It would have been midnight, when it closes."

"And what did you do then?"

Miserably, he said, "Well, we hung around for a few minutes – you know, saying goodnight – then we drove home. We both had cars there."

"Did you see her actually drive away?" Brett put in.

"Yes," he replied with a puzzled frown.

"As far as you could see, did anyone follow her?"

Lance shrugged. "A few cars left at the same time. Always do at throwing-out time."

"Was it a good evening, Lance?" Clare croaked. "Did she seem to enjoy herself?"

For an instant, Lance seemed to be lost for words. "She … er … yes, I'm sure she did." He wiped his face, holding back his emotion.

"You didn't have a row with her or anything like that?"

"No," he claimed. His face creased. He was on the verge of an outpouring of grief.

To take the heat off him for a while, Clare asked a more innocent question. "Did Nicola have her hair done recently? A trim, perhaps."

Swallowing back the tears, Lance looked blank. "Yes. Why…?"

Interrupting him, Clare asked, "Did she complain about it at all? Did she say it was a bad job?"

"No," Lance answered. "It wouldn't have been. She was a hairdresser herself and one of her work-mates did her hair."

"Did you come straight home after you left the club?" Brett enquired.

"Yes."

"And your parents will confirm it? Did they see you come in?"

Lance let out a weary and exasperated breath. "They were already in bed when I got back. It *was* after midnight," he pointed out.

"OK," Brett said. "I think you've had enough for now. Later today, you'll have a visit from someone who'll want to take your fingerprints. You see, we've got lots of prints from Nicola's car and the weapon. We want to exclude any that are yours so we can work on the others. Presumably your prints could be on her car. You *have* been in it, haven't you?"

"Yes. Quite a lot."

"Tell me one thing," Brett added. "How do you feel about going on the telly to make an appeal for information that'll help us catch whoever did this?"

Three of the four drivers who had seen Nicola's car in the slushy early hours of Wednesday morning added nothing to Brett's investigation, but, unwittingly, they became suspects. They provided Brett and Clare with three names to consider.

Andrew Laughton was a fifty-year-old golfer and insurance salesman who wore an expensive suit and an unlikely moustache. He had left the clubhouse at twelve-twenty. He'd promised his wife that he'd be home by twelve-thirty so he was clock-watching. Graham Maggert was a shift worker who always rode his motorbike along the A57 into Worksop just before one o'clock. He was coming up to his thirtieth birthday and he had convictions for shoplifting and motorcycle theft. Daniel Kolander was tall and thin, with short hair bleached strikingly blond. By trade, he was a lorry driver. Interestingly, like Nicola herself, he had been in Mixers on Tuesday night, but he wasn't acquainted with her. He was driving home from the nightclub when he saw her abandoned car. He was on the road much later than Nicola because, he said, he'd gone for a curry with friends after Mixers had closed. He'd noticed Nicola's abandoned Peugeot at one-fifteen. None of the three had seen any activity.

Ian Lowe was a different matter. The spotty twenty-three-year-old had helped to clear up at the clubhouse and left late – twelve-forty-five was his best guess. He'd turned left towards Sheffield and he couldn't be sure but he thought that the car in front of him had just accelerated away from where Nicola had been forced to pull in. While he spoke he stared intensely beyond Brett and Clare. With a serious stammer, he explained that he hadn't got close enough to identify the car. He'd seen only its taillights. It was neither a large nor a particularly small vehicle. It was being driven fast while Ian was taking it easy. By the time he took a right into North Anston, the car was no longer in view.

Clare got the clear impression that Ian Lowe was a bit of a loner. "He volunteered to tidy the clubhouse when the other guests had gone," she said to Brett after the interview. "I might be wrong but it probably means he ingratiates himself to win their favour – and their company. I bet the other members tolerate him more than welcome him. I feel sorry for him.

Low self-esteem and not exactly charismatic. Wouldn't make him the most popular person in the world," she commented. "Sad, really, but worth keeping an eye on. I'm not sure he was quite as weedy as he made out."

"Yeah," Brett agreed. "Being a bit weird's necessary, but not all it takes to be a murderer, though."

"He fits your theory about seeming to help the investigation only to make a game of it or to find out how we're getting on."

"True," Brett murmured. "If you're right and he knows the members of the golf club don't really want him, he might occupy himself with murder and the police instead. Even if it is dangerous. Anything for company if he's lonely. But let's not get carried away. Too much guesswork here for my liking. I'll tell you one thing, though," Brett added, "if all four are telling the truth, we might have the timing. Nicola leaves Lance outside the club just after midnight. Her car breaks down at about twelve-fifteen, say. First sighting five minutes later. Maybe Andrew Laughton didn't see anything because Nicola was crouching down by the flat tyre. There was no action at one o'clock or one-fifteen. That's because she was dead by then. How long does it take to stop, crack someone over the head and drag her body a few metres to nearby bushes? Five minutes? Ten minutes? So, our man stops at about twelve-thirty – maybe just after – kills her and drives off at twelve-forty-five in front of Ian Lowe. Or maybe Ian Lowe does the killing himself. Either way, it's consistent with the facts. Doesn't mean it's right but it's our best theory until someone disproves it."

"What next?" asked Clare. "Go and collect Lance ready for your big TV debut?" She looked at her watch and said with a devilish chuckle, "Six o'clock. Won't be long now. Local news tonight, *Miss Marple* tomorrow, *Prime Suspect* next week. Your Grammy awaits!"

"Any more heckling from you," Brett said, "and I'll fake an injury so you have to deputize."

"Me? A meagre sergeant? Besides, not with a red nose, blocked passages and a cough. I wouldn't be able to enunciate clearly." More supportively, she added, "I'll buy you an ale afterwards. Cheer you up."

"I don't think so," Brett retorted mischievously. "*I'm* going for a game of squash with a mate. *You'll* be answering all the calls from the public."

"Powder my nose?" Brett exclaimed.

"It stops the lights bouncing off it and making it look like a beacon," the woman replied.

Brett shrugged unhappily. "OK." Unwillingly, he submitted his face for the treatment.

Suppressing a giggle, Clare walked away. In an empty interview room she tried a decongestant on her own nose. It was like using a squirt of water to smash down a brick wall. She gave up and returned to the hubbub of the press conference.

Under the spotlights, shuffling uneasily, Brett squatted in front of a colourful cardboard display with the South Yorkshire Police logo and pictures of Nicola, her car and a local map. To make his sober appeal for information, he moved to a seat behind a bank of four microphones, a desk and a small sign bearing his name. Trying to eliminate the tremor from his voice, he gave a brief description of the case. Then he leaned towards the microphones and said, "I'm particularly keen to hear from anyone who saw a blue Peugeot parked by the golf course between midnight on Tuesday and one o'clock on Wednesday morning. We believe that someone in another vehicle stopped to help Nicola. I want to trace that driver because he or she may have vital information that would advance our enquiries. Please call us on 01142 669966 if you stopped that night or saw another car parked with Nicola's Peugeot. We're also anxious to trace Nicola's movements from midnight, when she left Mixers nightclub." He hesitated before adding awkwardly, "There's another angle we're pursuing. We believe the culprit would have returned home in the early hours of Wednesday morning in bloodstained clothing. If you know such a person – if you're protecting him or her – you should come forward and tell us. We'll take any calls in confidence."

Brett handed over to Lance Golby. On the point of sobbing, Lance wrung his hands as he added his faltering and emotional plea for help to catch his girl-friend's killer. He ended by spluttering, "I don't want anyone else to suffer like I am – and like Nicola did. Please, if you know something, tell the police before he does it again."

After a moment of respectful silence, the assembled reporters began to shout their questions at Brett. "How did Nicola die?"

"A blow to the head."

"With what?" came the gruff response.

Brett cringed as he quoted the traditional reply. "A blunt instrument."

"Have you found the weapon?"

"Yes," Brett admitted. "It came from the scene of the crime but we haven't finished examining it yet," he fibbed, "so I can't say any more about it at the moment."

"Was it a local man?"

Sweating under the heat from the bright lights, Brett responded evasively, "I'm exploring all avenues."

"What was his motive? Did he know Nicola, do you think?"

"I'm not ruling out any motive just yet."

"Is he likely to strike again?"

"There's no need to get hysterical about the threat but there's a chance he might try it again," Brett answered, not realizing how much he would be made to regret the statement later. "Lone travellers should be cautious if approached by strangers." Chillingly, he added, "We need to catch the person responsible as soon as possible."

By the time he'd finished answering questions – or dodging them – Brett realized that he knew very little about Nicola's killer. After the ordeal of the press conference, he assigned several members of his team to staffing the telephones from nine-thirty when his piece would be broadcast for the first time on the local TV news. Before his game of squash, he accepted Clare's offer of a drink.

In the event, though, they dashed out of the pub, leaving their drinks unfinished. A mobile telephone call informed them that the second set of fingerprints on the wheelbrace belonged to Lance Golby. Immediately, they drove at speed through the night of cold pelting rain to the Golbys' house.

"Just another couple of questions," Brett said to the troubled young man. "But first, thanks for this evening. Hope it wasn't too much of a trial for you."

Lance ran his fingers through his short hair and said, "It was OK. Let's hope something comes of it."

Clare let out an almighty sneeze. Both Lance and Brett turned and stared at her. "Excuse me," she mumbled.

By force of habit, Lance said, "Bless you!"

"Thanks," Clare muttered.

Lance added, "Hope you don't pass it on to me. I get colds really badly. One time…"

Clare looked at him strangely as he chattered on. A young man whose girlfriend has just been murdered should be preoccupied with his loss, she thought. He should not be concerned about catching a mere cold. She expected him to be more distant and distracted.

"Lance," Brett said, returning to business, "I've just had a report on your prints. Several were on the car, as we expected, but some were on Nicola's wheelbrace. Can you explain that?"

"Sure," Lance replied. "Last week, someone let one of her tyres down while she was parked in town," he grumbled. "I was with her. We didn't have a pump so we put the spare tyre on instead. I undid the wheel nuts."

"Which tyre?" asked Brett.

"Driver's side, back."

"OK. Thanks," Brett concluded. "I've got to check everything, you'll understand."

"Of course," Lance said agreeably, rising to see his visitors to the door.

While Clare drove towards her partner's house, Brett called Forensics again. "The wheels on the Peugeot," he began. "Any chance the rear driver's side was the spare until a few days ago?"

"Just a minute," the scientist said. He went to check his notes, or maybe to examine the vehicle again. Eventually he came back to the phone and reported, "Could well be. The tread on that tyre's much better than all the others and the metal inside is more corroded. That's what happens if, as a spare, it's been carried underneath the car. Consistent with that, the current spare isn't corroded but the tread's pretty worn. Yes, they could easily have been swapped recently."

"Pity," Brett replied glumly. "Thanks anyway."

"Bang goes our chance of an early arrest?" Clare queried.

Brett nodded. "Quite a coincidence. A puncture this week and a tyre let down last week. No way to confirm it but he might be telling the truth."

"I'm not sure about Golby," Clare voiced. "I'm not convinced by his grief. Before I turn in, do you fancy calling in at Mixers?"

"Dancing the night away in your state of health? You said you felt rotten." More seriously, Brett peered at his watch and then said ruefully, "Bang goes my chances of a game of squash as well. I'm not going to make it on time." He sighed. "OK, let's go and ask a question or two." He took the mobile phone again. "I'll call Phil."

"Phil?" Clare queried.

"Phil Chapman. A friend from university days, and mortal enemy on the squash court. I'll have to postpone the game."

Intense strobe lights provided a series of sudden snapshots of frozen action. Thunderously hypnotic music seemed to resonate within Brett's body. He smiled to himself. As he entered the club with Clare, they might as well have been wearing big signs with *Police Officer* written right across them. They stood out by being taller, smarter and older than most of the clients. They mingled but remained strangely apart. Killjoys. By shouting directly into the ears of the staff and the revellers, they asked a few questions but received little in return. The people in the club did not know Lance and Nicola or did not want to interrupt their own pleasure. The bar staff claimed to see too many punters to identify individuals. Yet Brett and Clare did not leave empty-handed. The bouncer on the door gave them what they wanted.

"You cops?" Jim mumbled.

Brett and Clare showed their warrant cards.

"And you're on about the one who got herself done in? The one on the news?"

"That's right."

"Well, I seen her. Her and her bloke." He stopped talking to examine a couple of female latecomers and search carefully through their handbags. His muscles strained the seams of his ill-fitting suit. When he'd finished, he said, "Club policy. Check for drugs. I've got to look in bags for little pills and stuff. With blokes, I've got to search 'em. That's because of you. Last week – Tuesday – you lot raided us."

"And we found something?"

"Not a lot. A few Ecstasy tablets. We're keeping our licence as long as we tighten up on searching."

"Glad to hear it," Brett responded. Trying to get him back on track, Brett reminded him, "You were telling me about the girl and her … bloke."

"Yeah. That's right. Night before last. When the snow was on its way out. What a row!"

"You mean, they were having an argument?"

"A cracker, to be sure."

"What about?"

"Don't ask me," Jim barked. "I see all sorts out here at closing time. You wouldn't believe it. Singles going out as pairs, all over each other in the street. Women telling the men where to get off. Scraps – I tell 'em to go further away to have their fights. Drunks staggering in the wrong direction, falling over, trying to get into taxis but missing the door. I've seen it all. I don't remember what they was shouting about but he went off one way, she went the other. In a huff. That's it."

"OK, Jim," Brett said. "That's enough. Thanks."

"Reckon he did her in?"

"You wouldn't have many customers left if they killed each other every time they had a quibble, would you?" Brett responded.

Jim laughed raucously and then bellowed, "That's for sure."

The storm cast cold raindrops that stung like the jabs of needles as Brett and Clare sprinted away from Mixers. Dripping in the car, Brett looked at his partner and said, "You look done in. Give it a rest till tomorrow. Let's go to my place. You can come in for a bit and I'll treat you to a hot drink – Lemsip or something…"

Brett's voice floated out from the kitchen. "I still haven't made sense of this Magic Eye picture you gave me. Annoying."

Standing in front of Brett's aquarium and watching the tropical fish glide and flash while Brett made coffee, Clare chuckled. "I got it for you because I'm taking an interest in surrealist art. It's a masterpiece, that one. Keep trying. It'll come." Then she called out to him, "You know, this is my first time in your flat. You've never invited me in before. Always preferred the company of your fish, I think."

Coming into the lounge with a couple of steaming mugs, Brett said, "Well, they are nice, aren't they? Calming." With a wicked glint in his eye, he continued, "And they don't catch colds."

"Not the best company, though," she observed. She sat down and sipped the coffee. "Mmm," she murmured. "That's good." She paused, wondering if she was about to be undiplomatic, but then said, "Would you call yourself lonely, Brett?"

"Lonely? Why?"

"Well, you collect fish and I always have this picture of people who collect things as rather lonely. Your parents are miles away, aren't they? And you said you've never got on with them. Then," she said, lowering her gaze to the carpet, "there was Zoe at Upper Needless. I know you cared for her."

Brett would not admit to the awful emptiness he felt when he thought of Zoe. "Not lonely, no," he declared. "With a job like ours I can't possibly be lonely, but it's tough to find the time for much of a life outside the force. Look what I've just done to Phil – stood him up. It's not the first time either."

Sometimes Clare also regretted that the job was all-consuming. "I dare say he'll forgive you, though," she said.

Brett laughed. "I wouldn't bet on it. At university, the two of us were on the same course and we always led the squash ladder. I don't think he's ever forgiven me for coming out on top in both. He's a good friend but sometimes I think he's still trying to outdo me. You know – reminds me how well he's doing in his job as a chemist and flings himself around the squash court like a madman, trying to beat me."

"And does he?"

Brett grinned. "Not usually," he said modestly. He took a drink and added, "I used to play a lot of rugby as well. Too busy now. Too busy to be lonely. Sometimes I wish there was someone here to come back to, but... Anyway, I'm not ready for the scrap heap yet. Besides, you're here, aren't you?"

"I suppose I was wondering why some lonely people become murderers. A form of attention-seeking, perhaps. I was wondering if it applied to our Ian Lowe. I bet he's a collector of something, and there's little doubt our man's collected a souvenir from Nicola. When we get him, my guess is we'll find a sad and lonely man. *You'll be getting to know me* – it's almost a plea to be noticed."

"Well, I may be a sad collector," Brett said with mock despair, "but I haven't resorted to murder yet." He turned away from Clare and gazed deep into the bright aquarium to hide from her the fact that, like yesterday with Anna Stimpson, suddenly he felt curiously light-headed and dizzy.

In the morning, Brett and Clare welcomed Liz to the case but did not brief her fully. Brett did not want to stifle her initiative. He gave her the bare facts of the murder – the offender traits – and let her loose on the computer. He needed her to find something but, at the same time, he feared what she might uncover.

Lance claimed that he hadn't mentioned his quarrel with Nicola because he was ashamed of it and because he didn't want to admit that he had a motive. Besides, it was only a tiff.

"A tiff about what?" asked Clare.

"Oh, you wouldn't understand," Lance groaned. "It was about who was dancing with who when I was left for ages like a lemon at the bar."

"I can understand jealousy, if that's what you mean," Clare said with compassion. She turned away, coughed, and then continued, "Nicola danced with someone while you were left on your own. We can understand it's perfectly possible – even in a crowd – to feel lonely," she glanced significantly at Brett, "especially when the only one you're interested in is having a good time right in front of you with someone else." At least Clare had learned why Lance's sorrow was not entirely convincing. A rift had opened up between them. Lance thought that he might lose Nicola even before she was murdered. "Who was he, this chap who danced with her?" she enquired.

"I don't know. Never noticed him before. He just swooped and asked her to dance. She agreed."

"Did he say anything to Nicola while they danced? Did she tell you afterwards?"

"No. She didn't say anything. But…"

"But what?"

"I saw him again. Later. He was acting suspiciously."

"In what way?" Clare asked.

"I don't know. But he was mixing with the wrong crowd, if you know what I mean."

"Drugs? Is that what you're saying?"

Lance shrugged. "Quite possibly."

Interested in his speculation but wanting him to keep to firmer territory, Clare said, "OK. But in the end, Nicola left with you, even if you did have a tiff about it. Might that have put this other man's nose out of joint, if he was after her?"

Lance shrugged again. "I don't know. I suppose it might. I didn't see him when we left the club."

"Could you describe him?"

Lance frowned. "Have you seen the lighting system in a disco? Either too dark or too bright in turn. Strange colours as well. Disorientating – deliberately for effect."

"What were your impressions of him?"

"A bit older than me, I think. Maybe your sort of age, mid- to late-twenties. Shorter than me. Thick-set. Short dark hair. I suppose he'd be called good-looking in a rugged sort of way. He had a T-shirt with a slogan across it – I couldn't read what it said."

"Was he black or white?"

"White."

"You should've told us about him before," Brett put in.

"It didn't come to anything."

"Little things can be important," Brett remarked. "Besides, it may not have been so little for him. Perhaps he was hurt, devastated even, when Nicola left with you."

"Is there anything else you want to tell us?" Clare prompted gently.

Lance shook his head. "I don't think so," he mumbled despondently.

Since Brett's presentation to the press, the team had been receiving phone calls at a steady pace. Only three showed particular promise and Greg and Paula had already followed them up. The woman who had reported that her drunken husband had arrived home, covered in blood, at two o'clock on Wednesday morning had neglected the fact that he'd tripped on the path and cracked his head on the doorstep. It turned out that the man who had informed them that he'd stopped to help a female driver with a puncture had done so on the A60 at Warsop – right time, wrong road, wrong place. The old couple who had definitely seen other vehicles parked by Nicola's car had got mixed up. They had seen them on Wednesday at one o'clock in the afternoon, not one o'clock in the morning, and most of them were police cars.

Another three people had called to confess to the killing. Two wanted to admit to a shooting and the other believed that he'd stabbed his victim. Obviously they had not been paying much attention to the details of Brett's press conference. Greg had taken down their names and addresses, thanked them and said he'd be in touch if he came across any evidence against them. "Sad people," he moaned. "They always come out of the woodwork after a media release."

"OK," Brett said. "No confirmed sightings – not yet, anyway. What does that tell us?"

"Our man's discreet," Greg proposed.

"Or he didn't use a car," Clare put in.

"It tells us we need Liz to come up trumps," Greg suggested with a grin.

"Let's drive out to the golf club," Brett said to Clare. "Find out a bit more about Ian Lowe."

"Good idea," she replied, keen to have him under the spotlight.

"You hold the fort, eh, Greg? If any more hopeful leads come in, check them out."

"All right," he agreed in a tone that suggested he

was resigned to failure. "I'll draw the line at alien interference, the appearance of Satan, or an MI5 cover-up."

The manager of the clubhouse shook his head sadly. "Tragic really, that one. You see, it was his father. Bit of an authoritarian, it has to be said. Used to be a colonel in the army. But Charles Lowe was a respected member of this club." He checked his watch, pulled a pint of lager and left it on the bar. Within a few seconds, a man walked into the room, strode up to the pint and took it, murmuring his thanks to the manager. "Ian was on the receiving end of his father's discipline. But, you know, if the boy had been OK, it wouldn't have done him any harm. Done him good in my view. Not enough discipline these days, that's the trouble. But Ian was never right. I think you know my meaning. When Charles died – mysterious circumstances I think is the phrase – the lad didn't have a direction any more. He went to pieces. Out of respect to his father, we allow Ian to be a member here but he's not really appropriate material. To be frank, Inspector, we suffer Ian in deference to his father. He was pitiful enough already, but without this club, I guess he'd have nothing at all. If it weren't for Charles, though, he wouldn't be … er… Let's just say he wouldn't be welcome."

All of a sudden, Clare felt even more sympathy for Lowe – and even more suspicious of him. He *was* a loner and he'd had a monster – a bully – for a father. No wonder he found it difficult to mix with people.

"When did his father die?" Brett queried.

"Not that long ago. In the autumn."

"And how did he die?"

"An accident it's said. He fell down the stairs."

"Which stairs?" asked Brett.

The manager frowned at him. "Not here. At home."

"I see," Brett said. "Thanks. You've been most helpful."

Before Brett and Clare could escape, the manager leaned over the bar and whispered, "You don't think Ian had anything to do with…?" He jerked his head in the direction of the eighth green.

"It's just one of many lines of inquiry," Brett stated.

When Brett and Clare returned to the police station, Liz was the first to call out to them. She was sitting at a computer, looking pleased with herself. Her long black hair was piled up on her head and fell down in chaotic cascades, like a fountain. Strangely, it suited her. "Have I got news for you!" she exclaimed. "Sit yourselves down and fasten your seatbelts. It's going to be a bumpy ride. I plugged all the details into the computer and—"

Excitedly, Brett interrupted, "You found some other cases with the same hallmarks?"

"In almost every respect, no. I've got two ongoing

murder cases, though. Two different locations, two different modes of killing. One strangulation and one drowning. One outside, one inside. Different ages, both female, like Nicola Morrison. One teenage girl, one old woman. Not much else matches. The girl was strangled at night in a park in Flint on the North Wales coast, the old woman was drowned in her own bath at night in Cheltenham, Gloucestershire Constabulary. Ironically, she was a good swimmer in her day, the report says. Anyway, there *are* similarities. In both cases, like Nicola's, there was no obvious motive. No robbery or assault. More interesting, the girl's fingernails had been cut. Her mother said she wore them quite long but when she was found they were short and jagged. Ten little mementoes?" Liz proposed harrowingly. "The old woman had false teeth and – you guessed it – according to the report, they were never found. Weird. Disgusting. And I found what you really wanted: a calling card was left with both victims. *I am somebody* – that was the message left by the old lady. Strangely, the girl had *She will help me.*"

"She will help me?" Brett could feel the adrenalin flowing through his body. It was stimulating and alarming at the same time. "I don't know what it means but that's our man all right. When did these murders happen?"

"The old lady in Cheltenham went first," Liz answered. "Christmas Eve. I don't suppose it helped her family's festivities. The teenager probably had the dubious honour of being the first murder this year: New Year's Day."

"I suppose I never got to hear about them," Brett said, "because the officer in charge of each case was keeping quiet about the bizarre bits."

Clare took the handkerchief away from her nose and commented, "Like you are."

"That's right," Liz responded. "Each force is keeping quiet about the peculiarities of its own killing. I had to dig pretty deep into each police file to get access to this level of detail. Easily missed. Of course, I can't rule out finding more. But, if there are more, each one'll come under a different police force, I bet. If any force had a second case to deal with, they'd have pushed the panic button by now. We'd have been alerted. At the moment, the different forces probably think they've just got a one-off. If it *is* one man behind them all, though, he's planning very carefully."

"Meticulously," Brett said. The notion of a devious schemer with inexplicable motives troubled him. He sighed. "Anyway, Liz, brilliant work as always, but I think we'll all have to call it a day now."

Clare and Liz frowned. "Why?" they chanted in unison.

"Because it'll be taken out of our hands," Brett explained. "It's not a South Yorkshire job any more, it's nationwide."

"Well, *I'm* not off the case yet," Liz exclaimed. "You two had better go and see the Chief but I'm still digging around."

Brett put his hand on her shoulder. "Good, but the Chief'll put the word round all police forces and any more cases will come to the surface anyway."

"Bet I'm faster," Liz boasted with a grin.

Brett nodded. "Very probably." Turning to Clare, he said regretfully, "Come on. Let's go and tell the boss. Do ourselves out of a job."

On the way to Keith Johnstone's office Clare said, "North Wales... You know who went there, don't you?"

A warm smile appeared on Brett's face. "The new Detective Chief Superintendent – John Macfarlane. He'll be in charge of the Flint case. I wonder what he made of it. It would've been good to pool his information with ours." Brett did not want to let go of the case but he knew that it was now too big for any one authority to handle. Reluctantly, he had to pass it back to the Chief.

With a wry expression on his face, the Chief Superintendent murmured, "It's always the same with you, Brett. I give you a tricky job and you confirm it's tricky. I give you a simple job and you discover that's tricky as well. I could give you a case of shoplifting or book theft, and you'd end up with a major inquiry, implicating the Prime Minister in multiple murder. Why is nothing ever simple?" He groaned audibly. "Ah, well. Keeps us in a job, I suppose. OK. Needless to say, you're off the job. I'll have to talk to all the chief constables and work out how we're going to tackle this one. Once I've contacted the other forces, I'll call you in again so you can add your information to the pool." Even before Brett and Clare had left his office, the telephone was in his hand.

As soon as Brett and Clare entered the redundant incident room, Liz called out, "Uttoxeter, Staffordshire Police. They've had one. Another woman. Another fresh air job. Found on some rough ground behind the parish church last week, a few days after she was killed. On the eighth or ninth of January, the pathologist estimated. One clean and accurate knife wound." Liz drew her forefinger graphically across her throat.

"Message?"

"*Make a name for myself.*"

"He's getting more cryptic."

"Don't forget the order of messages, Brett. So far, we've had *I am somebody, She will help me, Make a name for myself, You'll be getting to know me*. It's not more cryptic. Maybe more sophisticated sentence construction. That's all."

"I see what you mean," Brett said. "We're supposed to string the middle two together: *She'll help me make a name for myself*. He really is obsessed with being famous – or infamous – isn't he?"

"One thing's for sure," Clare put in. "He *wants* us to make the connection between his murders." Grimacing, she added, "Any souvenir taken?"

"You're not going to like it," Liz ventured. "He used the penknife again after she was dead. The

51

corpse didn't have its full complement of skin." She drew a square on her chest, ominously tracing the segment that the killer had removed.

"That's it, then," Clare muttered. "Until some major inquiry team needs to squeeze the juice out of us and then get on with the job on their own."

"Well…" Brett hesitated, "no one's told you to stop work, have they, Liz? So why not dig out all the details you can find on the accidental death of Colonel Charles Lowe, father of Ian? It happened sometime last autumn. You never know when we might need to know such things. As for us," Brett said to Clare, "we're on holiday. How about a little excursion?"

"Where to?" Clare asked suspiciously, sniffing and getting a handkerchief ready for a sneeze that did not come.

"I hear Uttoxeter's very nice at this time of year."

Clare warned him, "That's called encroaching on someone else's patch."

"Not if we're mere tourists," Brett countered.

Police procedure wasn't Brett's strength. He went about solving crime in his own way – like a scientific study. Driven by curiosity, he gathered facts, interpreted them and formulated a theory. Then he set about finding more facts that were inconsistent with his theory. If he found them, he had to ditch the theory and find another. At the end of the road lay the truth. He wasn't conventional but he got results, and he didn't want a little thing like geography to get in his way. His curiosity knew no boundaries.

St Mary's Church stood beside a busy street near the centre of Uttoxeter yet, as soon as Brett and Clare pushed open the gate and walked into its grounds, they seemed to enter a becalmed world. The noise of the traffic no longer reached their ears and shops gave way to the serene building and plain rectangular lawn. The off-duty police officers followed the path down to the sunken lawn, made soggy by the recently thawed snow. At the end of the grassed plot, there was a rough area. Somewhere among this mini-wilderness, a police dog had sniffed out the woman's defiled body.

Whispering, Brett said, "Amazing! We must be fifty metres or so from a busy road and we might as well be miles from anywhere. Silent. Secluded. Not overlooked."

Behind them, the blank back wall of the church separated them from normal life. Trees and bushes cushioned them on the other three sides.

"She probably came in for a bit of peace and quiet – a bit of solitude – not knowing *he'd* followed her in. Perfect place for a quick murder at any time of the day or night."

Clare sneezed and the surroundings deadened the sound immediately. "Different from the golf course but, in a way, similar," she observed. "Green and deserted, just off a main road."

"Exactly," Brett agreed. "It's got the feel of our man about it. Let's take a walk around, see what else there is."

As they walked away from the main shopping area, battling against the unpleasant winter wind, the road rose over a bridge. Underneath, to the left, there was Uttoxeter railway station. Once over the rail track, the road became more rural. Five minutes after leaving the church, Brett halted and pointed to the left. Just off the road there was a farm, Uttoxeter racecourse and a golf course. The northern boundary of the site was marked by the railway line and a brook.

"Am I imagining things," Brett muttered, "or does this look like the Worksop location? At the edge of that golf course, there was a canal and a railway."

"No, you're not imagining things," Clare reassured him, "but it might be a coincidence."

"It *might*," Brett agreed, "it might not."

"You mean, we've got a serial killer who travels from golf course to golf course by train?"

Brett shrugged. "Where's the nearest racecourse to Worksop? Doncaster?"

Clare nodded. "Twelve miles to the north – something like that."

"Cheltenham's got a famous racecourse. What about Flint?"

"No idea," Clare admitted.

"And are there golf courses at Flint or Cheltenham?" Brett asked rhetorically. Frustrated, he flung open his arms. "This is why we should still be on the case, us and Liz. We're beginning to see the links: women victims, calling cards, golf courses, racecourses maybe, railways, a busy road and waterways. They can't all be relevant but Liz could feed it all into a database and see what's common. If there really is a pattern, she'll spot it." He groaned aloud. "As soon as we're beginning to get a feel for him, we're taken off the case."

Clare squeezed his arm. "Come on. We've seen the Uttoxeter site for ourselves. We're not going to learn any more, we're just going to have more tantalizing thoughts that we can't follow up. It's annoying but we've got to give it all to someone else to look into."

In the car on the way back to Sheffield, Brett examined a road atlas. "Flint's got a railway station, a golf course and, ten miles along the river estuary, there's Chester racecourse."

"Add a demented jockey to the hit list," Clare returned.

Suddenly, Brett put down the road map and pronounced, "Next Thursday, the twenty-fifth! It's obvious. That'll be the next one."

"What?" Clare exclaimed, keeping her eyes on the road.

"He's killing once a week. If the Uttoxeter murder was the ninth – last Tuesday – he's on an eight-day cycle. His first strike was on the twenty-fourth of December and his second on the first of January. That's eight days, isn't it?"

"Sure is," Clare confirmed.

"Then the ninth and ours on the seventeenth. Every eight days."

"OK, it might be next Thursday. But where, Brett? And who?"

Dejectedly, Brett put in, "And why?"

Brett relieved some of his frustration in the morning by running hard around the park instead of taking his usual easy jog. Then he took a hot, vigorous shower. Before he set out for work, he hesitated by his aquarium. As always, the small guppies and tetras were running rings round the almost stationary discus fish. Brett wondered if the large placid discus could experience loneliness. It reminded him of a dejected Lance Golby, left at the bar, while the revellers flashed across the dance floor. He resolved to call in at the garden centre and buy a companion discus fish.

At the police station, Clare greeted Brett with the

news that the Chief wanted to see them both. "Pronto, he said."

Brett's eyebrows rose. "The big boys have made their decisions, then. Let's go and find out who we'll be replaced with."

Brett and Clare were in for a shock. Keith Johnstone announced that a high-power team would be assembled to undertake the investigation and that it would be headed by Big John Macfarlane, but the Chief Superintendent had decided that North Wales was not the best location for the squad. "He wants to base it here. We're more central and, John said, it acknowledges your work in connecting these four murders. You're going to have a busy day," he remarked. "John's arriving this afternoon. You two need to prepare as much as possible for a major investigation. There'll also be two officers, rank of inspector and sergeant, coming in from each region involved. You can keep your existing team intact as a service to this new squad and you'll get access to more beat officers. OK?"

Brett was in two minds. He could see himself relegated to the role of a worker bee to several imported queens, but he was grateful that he was keeping a fingertip hold on the case. "Does that still include Liz?" he asked pointedly. "After all, she was the one who tied the murders together, not us. And she'd be a real asset to the new team. She's the right person for sifting all the evidence from the different sites and finding common factors."

Keith smiled at his two young officers. "I don't think you fully understand," he said. "I have every respect for John. I value his opinions. You know that. If anyone can solve this case, he will. To do the job, he *insisted* that you and Clare join the team. He doesn't want you in the background doing the leg-work for him. You keep your existing team for that. He's requested that you two become his ... lieutenants. It's not a matter of you begging on your hands and knees for Liz, it's a matter of my needing to make her available to you because you want to commandeer her." Keith gave Brett a bruised smile and nodded. "I can spare her for the duration."

"Thank you, sir," Brett and Clare chimed.

"You're going to have to get used to your rank, Brett. If all goes well, you'll be a fully fledged inspector in June. Now's the time to start acting the part. And both John and I have high hopes for you, Clare. This case could be a springboard for both of you. So, go and set up shop," he ordered. "You have my permission to go out and buy yourselves a bigger wall-map."

Outside his office, Brett and Clare grinned broadly at each other. It was difficult for them not to cheer at the top of their voices, so they settled for a silent but triumphant fisting of the air.

"Just like old times," Big John commented as he lumbered into the incident room, handkerchief dabbing the perspiration from his forehead. He glanced round and remarked, "Too small a room, a serious lack of personnel, not enough computers, and a fast-track whizz-kid probationer in charge." While Big John grumbled, his bright eyes told a different story. He was pleased to be back.

Brett still felt in awe of the commanding officer in his first-ever case. The slow, self-opinionated, focused and colossal John Macfarlane was a force to be reckoned with. "Welcome back," Brett greeted him.

"I heard about your work on the Games case," Big John said unsentimentally. "In this business, when you become a star, it doesn't last long. You're only as good as your current performance. The slate gets wiped clean at regular intervals. Now," he said, "we've got serious work to do. Where's a decent sturdy chair for me? I sit, you brief me."

The investigation of the murder of Nicola Morrison exploded. Suddenly it wasn't a regional problem any more – it belonged to the nation. And the resource that was thrown at it reflected its new status. Brett had lost ownership of the case but he was still standing at the prow. The briefing room was awash with invading officers from other forces, telephones, faxes, and the pervasive smell of coffee. On the wall there was a large map of England and Wales, with four red pins marking the sites of the murders. Everyone in the incident room hoped that they would catch the culprit before a fifth dot was added but, privately and realistically, they all anticipated at least one more death before they had a hope of tracing him. Who was he? In the absence of a name, he became known as the Messenger.

In the middle of the hive, Big John was delivering his first briefing. The room was silent apart from the faint whirr of the computers, the squeak of polystyrene cups, the ringing of a telephone that Greg answered in a hushed voice, and Clare's occasional cough. "Now," John was saying, "you might think we're chasing a motiveless killer but, in my experience, no murder is ever truly motiveless. There's a reason all right but we haven't cracked it yet, or maybe it's so crazy only the Messenger can understand it. That means we haven't got inside his head yet. That's the missing angle. Once we get inside his head, we'll understand it as well.

"He's not committing murder randomly. For one thing, he's a once-a-week man – eight days to be exact. And it's not true that he doesn't have a hallmark. Sure, he changes his weapon, location and age of victim. It's unusual, but he's not random. He's only killing females. He's using a weapon from the scene of the crime each time: the penknife that his victim carried in her handbag, a bathful of water, a wheelbrace, and he's strangled with a scarf. So, he may not set out with a weapon, but he *does* set out with a calling card. He may not be armed but he's prepared to kill. And he takes a memento from every victim. Plenty of hallmarks, even if he's unusually liberal when it comes to choosing a victim, a place, a time of day and a weapon. Maybe he's an opportunist killer – he goes for it when the opportunity presents itself. Anyway, he's made no demands and his motive is obscure. Almost impossible to catch until we under-stand what's driving him to kill. So, I come back to getting inside him.

"What's significant about his eight-day schedule? Eight. The number of days that a police officer works each week? What else? We need to find links. This is where Liz comes into the picture. Liz, you've already got all the offender traits and forensic data from each death, haven't you?" Seeing her nod and murmur confirmation, John continued, "Good. Liaise with Brett over the forensic evidence. Now you need a list of everything distinctive within, say, fifteen miles of each murder site. I'll give you a list for the Flint murder, Clare can take care of the local one, and so on. We're already aware that golf courses, railways and racecourses might be significant. It'll be Liz's job to rule anything else out or rule it in. Once we see the links, it might tell us what's important to him. Then we're getting a bit closer to understanding his thinking, understanding what sort of person he is.

"Now, we all have our local suspects. Here, I understand there's an Ian Lowe, the victim's boy-friend – Lance Golby – and someone seen dancing with her just before she died. In Wales, the dead girl's called Leanne and I've got my eye on her uncle. The question is, do any of these suspects have motives for a wider killing spree and where were they on the days of the other deaths? We need a big push on that angle. Was Leanne's uncle still in Flint this Tuesday night and Wednesday morning, or was he near Worksop? That sort of thing. Brett'll organize his team to do the questioning of the South Yorkshire suspects. We'll be networked to similar small squads based in each region – won't we, Liz? – so us foreigners can organize similar trawls by our own teams back home." Pointing to a flip chart on his left, he said, "Clare's put up the details of each victim – best date and time of death – so you can see the movements that would turn a local suspect into a serious contender for all four murders.

"Now," John concluded, "I don't want the press cottoning on to the nature of this inquiry. I don't want any leaks. When they do realize we've got a big one on our hands, I'll deal with them. I don't want any unguarded comments reaching the media. OK, folks, introduction over. Time for action. Let's go get him."

"Brett!" Greg shouted. "Before you get going, there's someone you'll want to talk to – a charity worker down at Worksop's homeless shelter. He just phoned in as a result of your TV appearance. Claims he's got a regular – an old man – who's been wearing a bloodstained coat since Wednesday. Apparently he's a bit confused, can't recall where he got it from."

"Thanks," Brett said. "Sounds interesting. I'll make it the first call of the day."

The eyes in the old man's bearded face looked distant and a little scared. His hair was greasy, long and straggly. Apart from his coat with its brown stain down the front, his clothes were pathetically tattered.

"It's mine!" he burst out. He drew it tighter across his chest and hugged himself to prevent anyone snatching his prize possession from his shoulders.

"Yes," Brett agreed, "that's fine. But I'd like to know where you got it."

"It's mine. I found it. Finders keepers."

"That's OK with me," Brett said patiently, "but *where* did you find it? Can you remember?"

"It doesn't matter," the down-and-out said. "It's mine."

"It doesn't matter to you. It's still yours. But it'd be helpful to me if you told me where you found it."

The man's eyes darted suspiciously from Brett to Clare to the supervisor who had called them. "It could be very important, Bill," the supervisor put in. "They're not saying you did wrong, they just want to know where you found it."

"You're trying to take if off me," he uttered defensively.

Clare turned to Brett and said, "I'm going to leave you to it for a few minutes, OK?"

Brett looked puzzled but nodded and then spoke to Bill again. "I'd like to examine the coat for a bit, that's all. I don't want to take it off you. First, I need to know where you came across it."

Still clutching the coat possessively, the frightened old man glared at Brett without speaking.

"Did you find it in a bin?" the supervisor prompted.

Bill nodded.

"All right," Brett said, relieved that Bill had finally reacted coherently and helpfully. "Whereabouts was this bin?"

Bill whispered, "Wrapped in a plastic bag, it was."

"Whereabouts?"

"Behind the shops," he answered almost inaudibly. "Behind Woolworth's."

"Good. Was there anything else in the bag?" asked Brett eagerly.

"No, just a hankie."

"Did you take that as well?"

Bill shook his head. "A mess, it was. All dirty."

"Like this?" Brett went to point to the bloodstain on his coat but Bill staggered back nervously. "Never mind," Brett said. "When did you find it? Wednesday morning?"

Bill looked bewildered.

The supervisor intervened, saying, "Individual days don't mean much, do they, Bill? You've had it four days, haven't you?"

Bill shrugged and muttered, "About that."

Dreading the next part, Brett began, "Now, I really do need to check it over – not to take it from you. You can have it back but..."

Bill stared at Brett with defiance and determination. "No!" he barked.

The supervisor tried to help. "He just needs it for a few tests. There's no question about him keeping it, Bill. You'll have it back as soon as he's done the tests."

"No," he repeated.

"It's very important," the supervisor added. "Could be that someone's life depends on it."

"Not my coat," Bill snarled.

Coming back into the shelter, Clare said, "I'll swap it, then." From a carrier bag, she plucked out a brand-new, luxurious winter coat. She laid it in front of Bill and declared, "Best coat they had in the shop next door. It's yours for the one you're wearing."

Bill could not tear his eyes away from Clare's offering. "Really?" he mumbled.

"It's yours. Fair swap."

"No tricks?"

"None."

Bill felt the lining of the new coat and murmured to himself, "Warm." Suddenly, he grabbed it and stripped off the soiled coat. He held it out to Clare.

Clare turned the carrier bag inside out and held it open. "Just drop it in here," she requested. "I don't want to touch it – or let it touch where the new coat's been – because it might spoil the tests."

Bill hesitated, pushed his hand into one of the pockets of his old coat and yanked out a bottle of clear liquid. "That's mine," he muttered. He slipped the bottle into a pocket of his new overcoat and let go of the old one. Afterwards, he blurted out, "You're fools, you are! This is much better than that one. But you've done it now. No going back on the deal." He dashed away from them.

Brett grinned at Clare. "Good thinking."

"You men never think of the practical way out of a

situation. But you're going to have to be imaginative with the accounts when we get back. It cost me a fortune so it's going down on my expenses."

Before they took the stained coat back to Forensics, they paid visits to Lance Golby and Ian Lowe. No one answered at Ian's home but they found him clearing out a back room of the clubhouse. In his faltering, nervous voice, Ian claimed to stay at home almost all of the time.

"Ever been to the North Wales coast?" Brett enquired.

"N ... N ... North Wales? N ... n ... no," he said. "N ... n ... never." Obsessively, he scraped the dirt out from under each of his fingernails in turn. Even when they appeared to be perfectly clean, he carried on scraping with his thumbnail.

"I know you're a member here at the local golf club," Brett continued. "Do you belong to any other golf clubs?"

"N ... n ... no. Just this one. My father's." He hung his head and uttered the last word like a curse.

"Do you like horse-racing as well as golf?"

Ian was finding the interview very unnerving. He was sweating. "Horses? N ... n ... no. I've n ... n ... never been to a racecourse, anywhere." The tension made him pitiful.

"OK. Thanks," Brett said to end the exchange. He didn't want to prolong the torture for Ian. But he noted that, since Ian lived on his own, there was no one to confirm that he rarely left the house, apart from his visits to the golf club.

Lance Golby was very different. As a freelance computer engineer, he travelled widely, wherever there was work. "I don't usually go north from here. I'm best known from here to Manchester and the south. Not way south, you understand. I cover the Midlands."

"And Wales?"

"Yes," Lance admitted, "I've set up or fixed a few systems in Wales."

"Presumably it's not individuals who call you in, it's organizations," Brett guessed.

"That's right. I haven't done any work for the police yet," he said, trying to appear relaxed.

"Who, then?" asked Brett.

"All sorts. Councils, industry, even sports organizations."

Brett leapt at the opening. "Sports? What sort of sports?"

"Anything requiring computers. Athletics. I set up part of the Don Valley Stadium software in Sheffield. That sort of thing."

Clare interjected, "Golf courses?"

Lance shook his head.

"How about horse-racing?"

Lance frowned. "Yes, I've done a few. Why the interest?"

Ignoring Lance's question, Clare asked, "You didn't happen to set up Chester or Cheltenham, did you?"

"No. I've been to both, though, because I service

them when they've got a problem. I'm on call-out to quite a few racecourses."

"When did you last go to Chester?" Brett asked.

"Oh, I don't know. Some time ago. Last year."

"Presumably you keep a record of where you've been. Can we take a look? It's just a formality but it might help us with Nicola's case."

Unhappy with the direction of the interview, Lance grumbled, "I'll log on to my diary for you."

Lance's programme of visits was displayed on his portable computer. There were no entries for 24th December and 1st January. "What does it mean if a day's blank?" Brett asked.

"No work. Even a computer technician has a holiday now and again. I would've been here at home."

On 9th January, Lance had carried out some work for a management company in Wolverhampton. "How did you get to Wolverhampton?" Brett asked. "Across the Pennines and down the M6?"

"No. A38 via Derby."

"That would take you close to Uttoxeter," Brett observed.

"I guess so," Lance answered, "but I didn't go there."

"Mmm. Then, on Tuesday, you were here in Worksop with Nicola."

Lance nodded glumly. "I wish I'd been somewhere else, then we wouldn't have gone to Mixers. Then she wouldn't have…"

Clare said, "You might be interested to know,

Lance, that we've got a lead from your television appeal. You might have done some good for us – and for Nicola."

"Oh," he muttered. "That's good." Curious, he asked, "What have you come up with?"

Brett got to his feet, saying, "We're not sure yet so we're not at liberty to say. I'm sorry."

While Brett was being advised unnecessarily by the forensic department that any evidence from the coat had been seriously compromised because it had been worn for a few days by someone else, Clare was compiling a list for Liz. First, Liz wanted items in the immediate vicinity of the murder: the golf course, a canal (the disused Chesterfield canal), a main road (A57), the railway, a small river (Ryton), a farm. Then Clare listed features within a 15-mile radius of the spot where Nicola Morrison was killed: motorways (M1, A1(M), M18) and a motorway service station, a racecourse (Doncaster), an athletics stadium (Don Valley), several country parks, lakes and abbeys, professional football stadiums (Sheffield, Chesterfield, Mansfield, Rotherham and Doncaster). And so it went on until they had exhausted the characteristic landmarks.

After she had entered the complete catalogue into the computer, Liz recounted her research on Charles Lowe's fate. "Accidental death recorded. He fell downstairs in his house – more like a mansion from what I've read – after an evening of solid drinking.

Strangely, he was reputed to be able to take his alcohol without getting drunk and falling down a lot. Anyway, this time down he went. Hit his head on a wall at the bottom. His son, Ian, was in at the time but didn't witness the fall itself. At the inquest, it came out that Lowe Senior used to pull back Ian's bedclothes when he was young and beat him while he slept. At night, Ian is prone to panic attacks as a result. He's in a bad way, as far as I can gather."

"Mmm," Clare mused. "Makes you wonder, doesn't it? Beaten black and blue, Ian might have seen a way out. Just a simple little push when his father was sozzled and unsteady."

"There wasn't any evidence against him."

"No," Clare muttered. "But, if you met him, you'd see what I mean. His father's got a lot to answer for, I reckon. One wrecked son for sure."

Reporting to John Macfarlane, Brett and Clare admitted that they had nothing definite against Lance Golby or Ian Lowe. Equally, there was nothing that allowed them to be discounted. Lance's contacts with racecourses and his travelling were relevant to the inquiry but not necessarily incriminating. "Next Thursday," Brett noted, "Lance is going to Luton airport to install some new computer software. I sneaked a look while you told him about the response to his appeal, Clare."

Clare nodded and smiled. "I hoped you would. I knew the distraction would come in handy." To John, she explained, "Golby hasn't been totally honest with us. He didn't tell us he'd argued with Nicola. He might've been devoted to her but he could have flipped over a lovers' tiff. I don't know, but he's still on my list. And Ian Lowe's seriously disturbed, courtesy of an awful father. It's possible Ian pushed his dad downstairs and killed him in an act of retribution. I've got a lot of sympathy for him. Personally, I wouldn't blame him. Anyway, his father probably said he was a nobody so now he could be trying to make himself a somebody."

"Well," John said, "my Welsh suspect's got firm alibis for Christmas Eve and the ninth, so he's off the list. I'm still waiting for reports from the other regions. In the meantime, this overcoat's a good find. If the Messenger wore it and then dumped it because it was bloodstained, it's a dream-coat for us," John said. "Even if we didn't get it straight from the villain's back, it'll still have a story to tell." Addressing Clare, he asked, "This homeless chap – you're sure he's not a suspect himself? He was wearing the coat with the incriminating stain. He could've made up the story about finding it in a bag inside a bin."

"No," she answered confidently. "We checked him out with the shelter's supervisor, and we could see it for ourselves – George wouldn't harm a fly. Wouldn't have the wits – or a means of transport."

"OK," Big John replied. "At least we've still got *some* suspects on the list."

After finishing work on Saturday, Brett drove out of the city to the garden centre. For him, being surrounded by aquariums was usually a sanctuary from police work, from modern life. This time, though, there was no such refuge. A man was booming into a mobile phone as if it were a mega-phone and the person he was addressing was on the other side of the giant store. "They've got little ones with a nice bright blue stripe or others with an orange stripe. Yes. The orange stripe is nice as well. It goes all the way to the eyelids, making them glow. Looks like they've got shiny eye make-up. I can't make up my mind. Which do you think, darling?" He hesitated, listening to the response, then he bent down and looked into both tanks. "Both the same," he answered. "An inch at most, I'd say."

Eventually, the man said into his phone, "All right. Three of each, then. Yes. That'll be nice. As long as they don't eat each other. I'll ask if they mix first. If they don't, I'll call you back. All right, darling?"

Trying to ignore the intrusion upon the calm of the aquatic centre, Brett bought a young partner for his discus fish and hurried away.

As soon as he'd introduced the fish to his new home, Brett went to the sports centre for the re-arranged game of squash with Phil Chapman. As always, Brett won quite easily. Afterwards, over a drink in the canteen, Phil chatted gleefully about his work. "Oil," he proclaimed, "will run out around 2040, you know. Then what will you do for petrol in your car? Besides, petrol's mucky, polluting stuff. We'd be much better off without it. I tell you, Brett, I'm going to be the man who develops the alternative fuel. The man who, single-handedly, cleans up the environment. I'm well on course. Fame, fortune and fresh clean air are just around the corner."

"Good," Brett replied. "The next round's on you, then."

Phil laughed. "I said it's just around the corner – I haven't got it yet."

On Sunday, while they waited for results from forensics, Brett and Clare slipped out to watch Sheffield Wednesday get hammered. At half-time, Brett scanned the crowd and said, "You know, a lot of these fans go to almost every game. How do they find the time?"

"And the money," Clare added. She shivered inside her thick coat and blew her nose noisily.

"They travel all over the place, following the team. Roughly one match a week and it's not just Saturdays any more – Sundays and weekday evenings. Makes you think," he said significantly.

"Forget it," Clare said. "You're here to watch the game, to get away from the Messenger for a couple of hours. Besides, Flint, Cheltenham and Uttoxeter aren't best known for their football teams."

"Maybe Uttoxeter's on the way to Birmingham or Coventry. Maybe Flint's close enough to Liverpool. And Cheltenham… It's on the way to … Swindon or Plymouth."

"You're struggling," Clare observed with a grin. Clearly, she was feeling better. Even though she had not recovered her fitness, she had recovered her good humour. She had her cold on the run.

"He might not support one of the big clubs," Brett retorted. "It's worth looking into."

They were both standing, stretching their legs before the teams took to the pitch again. Squeezing up to let a couple of supporters return to their seats, Brett and Clare pressed inadvertently together. Brett murmured, "Sorry," but he wasn't really. He enjoyed the contact with her. Clare glanced at him, smiled and said nothing. She did not believe that there was anything to be sorry for. Perhaps she'd enjoyed it as well.

No matter how much Clare yelled in the second half, she couldn't resurrect her fading team. Football matches were like investigations, she thought. At the outset she always believed that there was a good chance of winning. Even after it became apparent that the opposition was strong, she still hoped that her team could snatch a lucky and probably undeserved victory. Sometimes, though, defeat was inevitable – the adversary was too cunning and cautious. Even so, Clare shouted encouragement to the bitter end. Three goals down and ten minutes to go, she was still playing her part in the game. She refused to trudge out of the ground downhearted and early. After the referee put an end to the slaughter, a disappointed Clare left Brett and went for a gentle swim. Normally, she would work out in the gym but, with the aftermath of the virus still gnawing at her, she didn't feel up to it.

Brett went home to see how the two discus fish were getting on. He hoped that they'd be swimming around like long-lost pals, like brother and sister, but they weren't. As always, his original discus fish was gliding serenely and proudly but the youngster was dead. The newcomer had been taught a territorial lesson by the old hand. He looked innocent and tranquil, incapable of cruelty, yet he had turned on the outsider. Of course, he was only doing what came naturally to fish. He had defended his stretch of water. He *was* innocent. Brett could not impose human values on his aquarium fish. They were what they were. Murder was not a crime among fish.

While Brett removed the victim from the aquarium

with a net, he felt unaccountably faint, as if he had suddenly become squeamish about death. His eyes saw the result of an aquatic squabble but his brain registered something much worse. He was forced to sit down. He buried his head in his hands and muttered, "What's going on?" When he next looked up, he caught sight of the Magic Eye picture through the open door of the kitchen. Still he could not make anything of it. It seemed typical of his life at the moment. He was receiving pictures, data, information, but they remained a mystery to him. He could not see the underlying meaning. He felt frustrated.

The initial results from the coat came in on Monday morning. On the phone, Greta from Forensics said, "One step at a time. The brown stain on the coat *is* blood. The Kastel-Meyer test was positive and spectroscopy detected haemochromagen. Is it human blood? A species test with anti-sera and electrophoresis shows it is. Our new fluorescent-antibody technique also confirms a human bloodstain," she reported. "Is it Nicola Morrison's blood? To be certain, you're going to have to wait for DNA genetic fingerprinting. For now, the blood group *is* identical to Nicola Morrison's."

Interrupting, Brett asked, "Level of confidence?"

"We matched the group, heptaglobin, transferrin and eight red blood cell enzymes. That's over 90 per cent confidence."

"Good."

"There's more. A few fibres we found at the murder site match the material of this coat, and a hair found on the victim's clothing matches a couple of hairs on the collar. More evidence that you've got the murderer's coat. Not that it does you much good. It can tell you something, I suppose, but not a lot. For example, the chemists found a trace of the drug Ecstasy on the right sleeve."

"Ecstasy! That's—"

"Almost worthless," Greta put in. "Maybe it got on there from the person who wore it last, like the other hairs we found."

"I know. I can't prove a thing, but Bill – that's the chap who's been wearing it – isn't the type for Ecstasy. Not exactly a party animal. Dodgy alcohol, maybe, but that's all." Brett continued, "I may not be able to prove that the wearer was inside Mixers nightclub a week last Tuesday, but I know there *was* Ecstasy in the club that night."

"There, and in lots of other clubs in lots of other places."

"True. I know it's useless for prosecution but it's not inconsistent with the owner of the coat having been in Mixers, like our victim."

"To make matters worse, it's a pretty common coat as well – nothing extraordinary. You'd get it from almost any high-street store," Greta stated regretfully. "Your firmest deduction is that your culprit is an average size male with average length dark hair."

"Thanks, Greta," Brett responded. "Ever helpful.

You've eliminated half the population, extremes in body size, albinos and bald people. We're down to forty-five per cent of the population."

Later in the day, John pooled all of the latest information. "The Gloucestershire brigade have got themselves a serious candidate," he reported. "A chap who travels a lot and is cagey about where he's been recently. He doesn't have alibis for the four murders. He does have previous convictions for assaults on women, though. Worth keeping an eye on. However, the prize goes to South Yorkshire with three suspects: Ian Lowe, Lance Golby and the unknown disco dancer. How are you going to get a handle on him, Brett?"

"A visit to Mixers nightclub tomorrow. There's a chance he might frequent it on Tuesdays. We've had reports of an Ecstasy find in the club a couple of Tuesdays ago and this chap might have been mixing with the users, according to Nicola's boyfriend, Lance Golby. On top of that, we've got Ecstasy on the killer's coat. Could be a connection."

"So, did the mystery man offer Nicola a little something while they danced? Was Nicola into the drug scene? Or Golby?" Big John enquired.

"Not as far as we know. No drugs found in her body. We haven't checked it out properly yet."

After his initial scepticism about a graduate entry, John had learned to appreciate Brett as an unusual but useful colleague. Even so, he took every opportunity to remind Brett of his inexperience. A smirk appeared on John's face as he said, "What are you hanging around for, then? Don't overlook the obvious in favour of a long shot. We need to find out if that's the link between the victims. It wouldn't be the first time drugs were behind violent deaths."

One of the Gloucestershire officers called out, "It's not very likely that our victim – the old lady in Cheltenham – would be into drugs."

"I agree," Big John responded. "But stranger things have happened. We need to consider *everything* in a case like this. If there's no drug connection, we'll dismiss it *after* popping a few questions in the right ears, not after thinking about it in this room. You see," he added, "there must be a reason why he picked those particular victims. Perhaps because they were available and vulnerable – no more than that. But what if it isn't? What if there's a real reason? We don't want to miss it."

Brett and Clare persuaded Lance Golby to go to Mixers with them on Tuesday night. They needed him to identify the mysterious dancer – if he was there. On the way to the club, Brett said, "There's something else I've been meaning to ask you. Did Nicola ever take drugs? Ecstasy, say, at Mixers?"

"Not as far as I know," Lance answered.

"And what about you, Lance? Are you involved in the drug culture at all?"

"No."

"Sure?" Brett checked. "I can get our chemists to

analyse your hair, hands, urine, clothes – anything – for traces of drugs, you know. The back seat of the car where you've been sitting. You'd be surprised how good they are at finding the smallest amount, long after you've handled or taken it."

"Maybe, but they won't find anything on me. Did they find anything on Nicola, then?" he asked.

"No," Brett admitted, "but I can't rule out a drug connection just yet."

Clare looked at Lance in her rear-view mirror. "New coat," she observed.

"Yeah," he said, looking down at it and stroking his left sleeve. "Christmas present from my parents."

"Nice," Clare murmured, sniffing.

At the door of Mixers, Jim the bouncer searched Lance while Brett and Clare watched. They suspected that their presence ensured a more thorough examination than normal. Inside, the club throbbed with drums and bass. Brett yelled into Lance's ear, "If you see him, point him out to me. Be discreet about it."

In reply, Lance nodded. He did not try to combat the volume of the music with his voice. He surveyed the mass of heaving bodies for a few minutes and then shook his head.

"Patience," Brett shouted. "Keep your eyes open."

Surreptitiously, Clare took up a position on the other side of the dance floor where she could see Brett and Lance. Sipping the drink that she held in one hand while drumming on the handrail with the other, she looked at ease – like a regular. Brett bought himself and Lance a drink and still looked out of place. He could not put out of his mind that he was in the club to do a job, and not to enjoy himself.

After forty-five fruitless minutes, Lance nudged Brett excitedly and nodded towards the entrance where a man had just come in. From his right thumb he dangled a coat over his shoulder while he scanned the crowd.

"Black jeans and orange T-shirt?"

"Yes, that's him," Lance said in Brett's ear, "the one who danced with Nicola."

"Stay here," Brett ordered. Then he glanced across at Clare and motioned with his head towards the newcomer by the door.

Clare understood at once. She put down her drink and closed in on the new arrival. She became one half of the pincer movement on the man who had danced with Nicola on the night she'd died.

The man in the bright T-shirt noticed Brett first. Instantly recognizing a police officer, he turned and made a dash for the exit. His coat flaring behind him, he swept past Jim at the door. With a curious frown, Jim watched Brett and Clare charge after him.

Clare groaned and coughed. *Now we'll see how healthy I am*, she thought to herself as the chase began. She doubted that she was healthy enough. Halfway down the main street, she learned that she was right. Her breath came in short, painful gasps and her throat and lungs were on fire. She flagged behind Brett and their quarry. The virus might have lost its tenacious grip on her but she had not fully regained her fitness.

Keeping his eye on the man and wishing he'd requested backup, Brett sprinted after him past the post office and shops. Without glancing back, he could tell that, for once, Clare was not keeping up. If she'd been a hundred per cent, she'd have been alongside him or even outpacing him. In her present state, he could not rely on her helping to corner the man he was desperate to question.

Ahead of Brett, the man darted into an alleyway that ended in a narrow lane behind Woolworth's. The dimly lit access road served the back entrances of the shops and was riddled with boxes, parked commercial traffic, bulging bin bags, crates and dustbins. By the time Brett hurtled into the service street, it was devoid of movement. The suspect had gone to earth in some dark recess or he had taken another passageway and eluded him.

Grinding to a halt beside her partner, Clare bent over and put her hands on her thighs. She wheezed and spluttered, then said, "Sorry. I'm not the woman I used to be. My arms and legs feel like lead weights."

"It's all right, not your fault. Two days away from the next murder," Brett muttered, "and I lost him! I should've anticipated that he'd be canny enough to recognize us as cops and make a run for it. I should've asked Notts for assistance – had extra people outside. As it is, we've only learned one thing."

Clare straightened up, took a deep breath and said, "He's got something to hide from us."

"Precisely," Brett agreed.

"You could call for backup right now and…"

Clare fell silent as they both heard a clattering noise from behind one of the large bins by British Home Stores. Clare glanced at her partner and together they began to patter softly towards it. Brett pointed to the left, indicating that Clare should approach from that side while he took the right. Cautiously, they parted and crept forward without another word. In the moment of hesitation before they pounced, a rustling from the other side of the bin confirmed that he was still there.

Brett took a deep breath, darted round and immediately sighed. A wry smile came to Clare's face. She recognized the coat of the man who was standing on a crate and leaning over the edge of the waste container. "Hello again, Bill," she said. "Still on the lookout for a good find?"

Bill's head materialized above them. He looked down at them with frightened eyes and mumbled defensively, "I ain't up to no harm." Wearing his brand-new expensive coat, he looked out of place as he scavenged for morsels cast out by the shops.

"Hope you're not getting that overcoat mucky," Clare said good-humouredly.

"You're not having it back. Deal's done."

"No, there's no problem with the coat. It's yours," Clare assured him. "We just wanted to ask you something else. Did you see anyone run past here? Just a minute or so back."

"Me? I seen nothing." It was the reflex action of someone who was determined not to cooperate.

All three of them stared up the access road as the intrusive headlights of a panda car came into view. It came to a sudden stop by the big bin and Constables Law and Jenson jumped out energetically. When they saw Brett, they slowed up. In answer to Brett's puzzled expression, Constable Law said, "We got a report of a chase going on. A possible fight."

"Yes," Brett responded. "It's over now, and no fight. We didn't find who we expected. He's long since gone, no doubt."

The policeman nodded at Brett and then looked up at Bill, who was still tottering on the crate. "Well now, Bill. What are you up to here?" He said it as if his local knowledge of the streets and the people on them would soon defuse the situation.

"I'm making a complaint, I am," Bill declared.

"Oh? What's that then?"

Bill stepped down from the box and, casting a sly glance at Brett and Clare, said to the policeman, "Against him and her." He pointed to Brett and Clare from a safe distance. "Harassing me, they are."

"Oh Bill, I don't think you want to do that," the constable replied. "They're the top brass, you know. If you complain, you'll have to go down to the police station, sign statements and all, and lots of top people'll need to quiz you. Do you really want that?"

Bill glanced again in Brett's direction and then shook his head.

"Best if you just be getting along. Maybe you ought to be going to the shelter."

With a look back like a wounded animal that had just escaped capture, Bill hurried away as quickly as he could.

Constable Law looked proud of himself. He turned to Brett and said, "Well, that's that taken care of. You can get on with more important things." There was a hint of a sneer in his voice and he wore an easy, quirky smile as if he had every confidence in himself and none in the CID. "Still on the golf-course case?" His tone implied that, if he'd been in charge of the investigation, it would have been completed by now – and he would certainly not have let a suspect slip through his safe fingers.

Brett nodded. "Yes." He didn't feel like expanding or explaining the complications.

"This time, it's your turn to be out of your area."

"Yeah. Chasing a suspect in the 'golf-course case', as you called it."

"You should've asked for our help," Law pointed out, "then you'd have got him."

More amiable and genuinely interested, Louise Jenson asked, "Did you speak to Anna Stimpson, the woman who called us in?"

"Yes," Brett answered. "We haven't ruled her out

but she seemed above-board. Besides, we're almost certainly looking for a man."

"How do you know?" Louise enquired.

"We've got the coat that the killer wore. It's a man's."

Louise replied, "I've got several female friends who wear men's coats – it's a fashion statement." As soon as she'd finished speaking, she looked faintly embarrassed at her presumption.

Clare put in, "No, you're right. It's a possibility at least."

Louise smiled but it wasn't a confident smile. She avoided eye contact with Brett or Clare.

On Wednesday night, all of the police officers in the incident room were on edge. The tension was tangible. They knew that they were waiting for another murder before they had a chance of progressing the investigation. Within twenty-four hours, they expected another corpse, sacrificed to the investigation, and another set of clues. The inevitability weighed heavily on them.

Big John was the most irritable of them all. "We don't have the resources to follow our suspects properly for a day from midnight," he grumbled. "When one of our targets starts to move, we'd need between five and ten cars and about thirty people on the ground to tail him without him knowing about it. We don't have that sort of backup. We already know Lance Golby will be driving out of the region and there may be others on the road as well. We're stumped."

Not even Liz could help them to prevent the fifth death. She had some common links but she could not narrow down the next site. She could not suggest a place to saturate with officers. There were just too many areas near a golf course, a waterway, a main road or motorway, a racecourse and a railway. Having scoured maps for the locations of golf courses, she was beginning to think that there might not be a golf course connection at all. Almost every reasonably populated region was within fifteen miles of a golf course, if not two. It could be a coincidence. Instead, Liz remained on-line to all forces, foraging for reports on incidents anywhere in the country.

The members of the team sat dismally and drank coffee and talked and complained, waiting for the Messenger to deliver his next deadly note.

Liz raised the alarm at nine-thirty on Thursday night. "We've got something in Cambridge," she announced, breaking the stalemate. "Someone killed this afternoon a few miles to the north of the city – a place called Girton. And guess what? It's just off the busy A14 and fifteen miles along it one way there's Newmarket racecourse. Fifteen miles the other way there's Huntingdon racecourse. The victim was shot on the provincial golf course. Hold on to your hats – there's a big shock coming. It was a man this time."

"A man?" John exclaimed.

"That's right. In his fifties. Out practising his swing. There's a calling card but Cambridgeshire Constabulary haven't put the message on file yet. You'll be interested in this, though: there's a first-hand witness. Some retired rower gave chase but the attacker got away."

"So," John muttered, "he may be fallible after all. Tomorrow morning," he said to Brett and Clare while he picked up the phone and dialled Cambridgeshire Constabulary, "you two come with me. We're driving to Cambridge."

Peter Colburn had been rehearsing his strokes on a sodden and secluded tenth hole. He had been shot twice by a point-two-two multi-shot handgun. The first shot, fired from a short distance, passed through his heart and killed him. To make sure, he was then shot through the head at very close range. Now the area was cordoned off and a tent marked the spot where Peter played his last stroke. Divers were searching the nearby pond and a line of officers were scouring the rest of the course for the gun.

The four detectives looked skywards and cursed. The bloated clouds that formed a bleak, claustro-phobic ceiling began to release their load. Only Big John had a coat with a hood. He pulled it up and ignored the discomfort of his young assistants and the local inspector. John turned to the Cambridge-shire officer called Nick and checked again. "You say the victim, his family and friends don't know anything about guns. He wasn't in the habit of carrying a gun illegally?"

"No. We're sure the killer must have brought this one with him. It makes sense, you see. He came with a calling card so he must've set out with the intention to murder. Obviously, he'd carry a weapon."

"Mmm," John mumbled. He hadn't yet come clean about all of the details of the other cases. "Logical," he replied, "but not our man's modus operandi."

The Messenger had changed two of his trademarks. This time the victim was male and the murder weapon was not from the scene of the crime. Big John looked down the fairway and said, "He had the means to use the same MO. Why did he import a weapon when he could've done the business with a driver or a three-wood? Why didn't he use one of the chap's clubs as a weapon?" Answering himself, he muttered grimly, "He's changed his routine because he's playing with us."

The Messenger had made sure the police would know that the murder was his handiwork by leaving another message made from press cuttings. Out of the cold and rain, back in the Cambridge headquarters, the local officer hesitated before he handed over the piece of card sealed inside an evidence bag. "We didn't understand this at first. Now I've been introduced to you," he said darkly to Brett, "it makes some sense."

Brett went cold when he saw the calling card. It hit him like a vicious punch.

LAW less on TV. soon it WILL be me

Dispassionately, Big John announced, "That confirms it. He's using victims to toy with us. It's becoming a sport to him. Mostly, Brett, he's toying with you – and that's dangerous. He might be starting to murder to antagonize you or – even worse – to impress you."

Unwilling to admit it himself, Brett tried to cast doubt on John's deduction. "It's only that he knows I'm on the case, through the TV appeal. He might've picked you if he'd known you're in charge of the case now, but he doesn't. Or he does but he won't admit it because it's not public knowledge yet." It was useless, Brett knew. No amount of wriggling could deny the inevitable conclusion: the case had become personal. In a way, the Messenger was killing for Brett.

Suffering in her damp clothes, Clare coughed. "One thing's for sure: he watches Yorkshire telly."

"In the north of East Anglia," Nick interjected, "it's easier to pick up Yorkshire telly than Anglia, but here in Cambridge, Anglia's the norm."

"With cable or satellite dish, almost anything's possible," John remarked.

"Lance Golby was in Luton yesterday," Brett reminded them. "How far away is that?" he asked Nick.

"Thirty, thirty-five miles. Something like that. Easy by car."

"Interesting," John murmured. Then he changed the subject. "What do we know about the Messenger? One: he's clever and unbelievably callous. Two: all he cares about is himself. He certainly doesn't care about the people he kills. They're just the disposable tools of his trade. Like footballs, he's going to kick them around as much as he likes, and we're letting him win every game at the moment. Soon, we've got to put a stop to his run or he'll win the entire match. Three: he's varying his MO now to impress us with his versatility. I think I'm beginning to see inside him but, when we get back, we'll have him profiled anyway."

In Terry Purcell's cabinet and on his wall were the testimonials of a successful career in rowing: shields, gold medals (including two from the Olympics), a Sports Personality of the Year trophy. His body was also a testimonial. He stood as tall as Brett. At the age of forty-eight, he still had broad, powerful shoulders, big, strong hands and muscular legs. These days, he was more likely to be seen at Huntingdon racecourse than on the river but obviously he still looked after himself. Brett thought that he might be seeing himself in twenty years. He knew Terry by sporting reputation and admired him in the way that he admired anyone with the dedication and motivation to reach the top – to be the best. He also wondered whether a man who had been so accustomed to the limelight could ever adjust to the quiet life of retirement.

"I was out walking my dogs across the rough of the golf course," Terry explained. He was sitting on the sofa with copies of *The Sporting Life* and *Racing Post* on the cushion next to him. "I heard the shots and saw someone kneeling over what I took to be Peter—"

"You knew Peter Colburn?"

"Yes," Terry answered. He sighed heavily. "Not a particular friend but a neighbour. We chatted now and again. He was in the Royal Artillery once, that I do know, and I've played a round or two with him. He was golf crazy. Wind, rain, anything, he'd be out on the golf course, improving his swing or his putting." He shook his head. "I'll tell you what, though – when I went up to see what was going on, I hardly recognized him. He was almost bald! I thought he had a good head of hair, but he must have worn a toupee. I never knew that."

Immediately, Big John turned to Nick and asked, "Was a toupee found at the scene?"

"No."

John glanced at Brett and Clare. They knew that the Messenger had another memento for his collection.

"OK," John continued, "what happened next? You went up to Peter's body. What was the other man doing?"

"He'd seen me coming and run off. When I realized Peter was dead, I chased him but… In my younger days, I'd have got him. He had a good start on me, that was the trouble. I almost caught him up but I couldn't keep going. He got away from me."

"Are you absolutely sure it was a man?" Brett put in.

"I only saw a back view but, yes, I think it was. Short hair, biggish build, and he sounded like a man."

Brett and John pounced at the same time. "He said something?" they asked eagerly.

"Not really. Puffing and panting, as you'd expect. And he … made noises."

"Noises? What sort of noises?"

Distressed, Terry said, "I think he was laughing."

Terry gave them a barely helpful description of the man that he had chased: average height, straight dark hair, average build, slightly thickset, jeans and dark coat. No idea about age. Brett thought about the disco dancer that he had pursued. It could be the same man. It could be a million others. They established that Terry gave up the chase near a small road that led to the A14 in one direction and the A1307, a main artery into Cambridge, in the other. It was likely that the Messenger had got away in a car that he'd parked in the lane. Brett was surprised that a former athlete, famed for his stamina and strength, had given up the pursuit. After all, he had kept himself in trim.

Big John levered himself out of the armchair but before they left for Sheffield, Brett said to the retired rower, "I see you're into horse-racing now." He glanced at the two newspapers on the sofa. "Do you go to different courses, following the horses?"

Terry looked puzzled but answered, "Yes. Quite a bit."

"Newmarket?"

"It'd be a bit daft going there now. Rather dull. The flat racing season's March to November."

"Over the jumps, then?" Brett checked. "Cheltenham, say."

"Of course. It's the Mecca of steeplechasing. Huntingdon, Ascot, Doncaster, lots of others as well. Why?"

"I just wondered how you filled in your time now," Brett responded. "It must be odd to dedicate so much time to a single-minded goal, to be a public figure, a hero, and then to drop it."

Terry smiled. "I don't know about hero," he said, "but there *are* other challenges now. Not lesser ones, just different. I'm a business consultant, I travel about a lot and I own a couple of thoroughbreds."

Clare watched him closely. Behind his grin she thought that she detected grievance and regret. She guessed that his current challenges did not have the appeal of fame and glory. She had a hunch that he longed for celebrity status again.

John curtailed the conversation. He thanked Terry for his cooperation and left. In the car, he explained, "I don't think today's the right time to turn a witness into a suspect."

Brett objected, "We could have checked his movements."

"And if he's the Messenger, he's going to admit, 'Yes, I was in Cheltenham on Christmas Eve and at New Year I went to Chester. A week later I went to Uttoxeter races and then Doncaster,'" John responded cynically. "He's seriously famous, Brett. We don't have to ask him and risk getting lies. We check the timing of races at the various places and we ask at the racecourses. Course stewards will know if he was there. And, Nick, check if he's into shooting, will you?"

"We already did," Nick replied in a self-satisfied tone. "He's into quite a few sports. He's a member of the local gun club."

"And I don't suppose the gun club will admit to losing a firearm, even if one's gone missing," John grunted.

"They reckon their security is up to scratch. All guns accounted for."

"They would say that, wouldn't they?" John muttered. He turned in his seat and the whole car seemed to lurch with him. He looked at Clare in the back and said, "Well?"

She sniffed and then gave her opinion. "I wouldn't discount him. Strikes me he's not really come to terms with being anonymous again, despite what he says. I reckon he's missing the telly interviews and being splashed across the newspapers."

John nodded. "Back page or front?"

Clare shrugged. "No idea. I suppose he'd rather hit the sports headlines again – perhaps that's what the horses are for. But then the jockeys and horses themselves get the glory, not the owners. If he can't get on the back page, perhaps he'd go for the front. But…"

"What?"

"He doesn't seem nutty enough."

Big John laughed. "The Messenger's got the type of nuttiness you don't see at first. If he acted nutty, we'd have him by now." He twisted in his seat again and said to Nick, "Well, I hate to deprive you but I think you have to hand the reins over to me on this one."

Nick breathed a sigh of relief. "Something tells me not to be disappointed."

John didn't like Nick's reaction. A good copper should relish the tricky cases. He did not request Nick's attachment to the core team in Sheffield. "All I need," John said, "is your cooperation. I need to take the calling card and copies of all your notes. If you find the weapon, trace anyone else who saw the car, get any results from the usual enquiries, let me know."

By Monday morning, 29th January, another pin had appeared on the large map in the incident room. It was a blood-red blot over Cambridge. "Right!" Big John shouted, instantly silencing the room with his vehemence. "I want results. Let's remind ourselves of our task here. Let's remind ourselves just how important it is to get him. I want big copies of all his messages up on the wall – an ugly reminder of his handiwork. And I want details of time, place, methods and his souvenirs up on the whiteboards. I don't want us to forget he's stabbed, shot, battered, drowned and strangled so far. He's got fingernails, skin, hair, teeth and a wig to prove it. He's got to be stopped." He took a deep, wheezing breath. "Liz, what do we know about the Cambridge calling card? In fact, remind us about all the newspapers he's been cutting up."

"OK. Forensics have identified them all now. The words have come from all sorts of sources, all sorts of newspapers. In order, it was the *Daily Mirror* and the *Daily Mail* in Cheltenham, *Angling Times* and *News of the World* in Flint, just *The Sun* in Uttoxeter, the *Daily Telegraph* and *The Times* here in Worksop, and now the *Guardian* and *Melody Maker* – would you believe? – in Cambridge."

"*Melody Maker*?" John thundered. "What's that?"

Brett enlightened him. "A paper on rock and pop music."

"Mostly a young person's paper," Clare put in significantly.

"Widely read, isn't he?" Liz commented.

"I don't think so," John replied, "and I don't think he's necessarily young. There's a possible fishing connection, as well. We've got the murders by waterways and the *Angling Times*, but I think it's all part of the game he's playing with us. It's more likely he lives near a good newsagent or visits good news-agent's on his travels. There *is* something you ought to look at, though, Liz: horse racing. Apparently there's a difference between courses. At the moment, flat racing's out. The gee-gees go over fences at Cheltenham, Doncaster and Huntingdon, I'm reliably informed. What about Chester and Uttoxeter? Do they go in for the jumps? Shouldn't be difficult to dig out the information. And did any of them have races on the days of the deaths?"

"I'll find a horse-racing fact-file somewhere and no doubt there'll be race schedules. Bet it's all on the Internet. I'll get some tips while I'm in there."

John ignored her humour. "If our man strikes when steeplechase courses are active, we'll need to send teams to each course. They'll find out if Terry Purcell was around at the time – and check on other regulars. And you'd better find which courses have got races on Friday or thereabouts. That's his next strike day if he keeps to his MO."

Interrupting, Liz glanced at Brett and Clare and then asked, "Want me to answer this? An E-mail's just come in." When John manoeuvred himself to her side, she pointed to the terse message that had been sent to all divisions of Nottinghamshire and South Yorkshire police forces: *I am anxious to speak to the officers who tried to interview or arrest a man at Mixers nightclub in Worksop last week on Tuesday night*. It had been mailed by Detective Chief Inspector Smith of Nottinghamshire Constabulary's

Drug Squad. He was based in Worksop.

"Yes," John said. "Tell him I'm anxious to speak to him as well. Tell him I'm on my way with the officers concerned."

He didn't get there. On the way to the car park, his mobile phone squawked insistently. It was his own chief constable and he wanted John back in North Wales immediately. A couple of hours previously, the Messenger's sixth victim had been found in Oswestry.

"What?" John exploded. "We're not due another one till Friday!"

"Well," the Chief Constable stated, "either he's lost his personal organizer or he's playing games with you. But you'll want to see the message. It could be the end."

A furious John put his head round the door of the incident room, delivered the unexpected news and announced his intentions. Before he disappeared again, Liz reported, "Uttoxeter's a direct hit. Steeplechasing under National Hunt rules, it says here, all year round. But no joy at Chester – the smallest racecourse in England and dedicated to flat racing. Twenty miles down the road from Flint, though, there's Bangor-on-Dee. It's little more than a steeplechase course as far as I can see."

"Bangor-on-Dee?" John uttered. "That can't be far from Oswestry."

Greg Lenton examined the map. "I'd guess … ten miles. That's all."

Big John sucked in air. "Get on to Cambridge, Greg. I want to know where Terry Purcell is right now. Someone else try Lance Golby. Where is he? Liz, what about dates of races? Do they coincide with our murders?"

"I don't know yet. More digging needed."

"Get on to it, then," he said. "I'm off to Oswestry with Brett and Clare. Call me on the mobile with any results." In the car, he mumbled to Brett, "Damn him! He's breaking his offender traits left, right and centre. He's not insane – he's highly intelligent, arrogant, and he's trying to make fools of us."

Brett was tempted to say that he was doing a pretty good job but, given Big John's mood, he decided against. Instead, he studied the road atlas and thought about the links. Oswestry had everything: a golf course to the south, the Shropshire canal and a steeplechase course to the north, the Shrewsbury-to-Wrexham railway line to the east, several small rivers and the main A5 from the Midlands to Anglesey. The chances that six murder sites would have all of these factors in common were slender. Brett believed there could be two reasons why a killer would chose such locations. They were part of his make-up. Maybe he did travel to racecourses like Lance Golby or Terry Purcell, maybe he liked fishing, maybe golf was his game, but maybe he was playing an altogether different game. Brett wondered if the Messenger had planned his crimes carefully to lead them to the wrong deductions. "I can't help feeling we're being manipulated by this man," he said. "I think he wants us to make the connections *he's* concocted – and it's working."

John looked askance at him and his black mood shifted a little. "Good grief, Brett. You almost sound like a police officer rather than a scientist."

Brett took it as a compliment. "Do you mean you agree?"

"My bones tell me there's a link we haven't got to grips with yet. These victims must share something that we haven't spotted."

Rain lay on the windscreen like a dreary blanket until the wipers brushed it aside. To lighten the mood, Clare put in, "I don't believe he's a jockey, anyway. The coat we've got would swamp a jockey. They're tiny things – like gnomes, not average height and build as Purcell described him."

Liz phoned with news from headquarters. "There were races at Cheltenham just before Christmas – that's one match. But there's only one other: the Uttoxeter incident happened a day before some racing. That's your lot."

"What about Golby and Purcell? Did Greg get anywhere?"

"Cambridgeshire can't find Purcell. He's certainly not at home and no one knows where he is. Golby's supposed to be working in Telford today, according to his parents – not a million miles away from you. I tried Ian Lowe as well. Called him at home and at the Worksop golf club. No answer from home and he wasn't at the clubhouse. It doesn't square with what he told Brett – that he hardly ever goes anywhere apart from the club. The Gloucestershire brigade say their suspect's just got home. Claims to have been in the Midlands, but he lives eighty miles south of Oswestry – under two hours by car."

"Thanks, Liz," said John as he ended the call. For Brett and Clare, he summarized, "No strong link with horse-races and no alibis for any of the suspects."

Brett was still contemplating the Messenger's cunning but he kept his conclusion to himself. If the Messenger was so successful at manipulating the reactions and deductions of the police, he had a good feel for the force's MO. He was able to steer the thinking behind the enquiries. To see the link that the killer was hiding, Brett might need to step outside normal police procedure. He had to see what was really there and not the obvious pattern that the Messenger was presenting. His restless mind drifted to the Magic Eye picture attached to his fridge door at home.

If Michael Black had fitted an efficient catalytic converter to his car, he might have survived. But his old car had no means of removing the carbon monoxide from its exhaust fumes when the Messenger tied him firmly into the back seat, yanked his spectacles from his face, dropped a calling card on to the driver's seat, opened the car windows, and left the engine running in the closed garage. With the exhaust issuing three per cent carbon monoxide, the atmosphere reached a lethal level in just ten minutes.

Michael was a chemist. He knew exactly what was going to happen to him over the next few minutes. Helpless and terrified, he could only wait for oblivion. First, he experienced a headache and mild nausea. As the concentration of carbon monoxide increased stealthily and displaced life-giving oxygen from the haemoglobin in his blood, he felt drunk and then faint. His eyes ceased to focus, he became weak and he slid into inevitable stupor, coma, cardio-respiratory failure and death. By the time that he was found in the smog-filled garage, his entire body had an unnatural cherry-pink tint – the colour of carboxy-haemoglobin. At post-mortem, all of his internal organs would also be pink. There would be pulmonary oedema and degeneration of part of the brain. Spectroscopic analysis of the blood would reveal sixty per cent saturation with carboxy-haemoglobin. A classic, clear-cut and simple poisoning by carbon monoxide.

The message on the calling card was short and mysterious.

i am compl*ete*

"What does that mean?" John spluttered.

Clare shrugged. "Has he finished his killing spree?"

Observing her, John surmised, "You don't believe that – any more than I do."

"No," she admitted. "I don't think he's finished.

He's hooked on killing. He's enjoying himself too much."

Brett looked closely at the calling card. "All the letters are in the same font and the paper looks the same," he noted. "Taken from the same source."

"So?" John asked.

Brett confessed, "I don't know, but we haven't put much effort into understanding the significance of the newspapers used yet."

"Unlikely that there is any," John retorted. "He's just messing around."

"You said you thought there was a missing link between the victims," Brett said to his chief. "I'm not so sure – but there's something about four of them, you know. The old lady in Cheltenham was a swimmer in her younger days and she was drowned. Nicola Morrison was a hairdresser and she was killed by a head wound. The Cambridge victim was in the Royal Artillery before he was shot. Now a chemist's been poisoned. Coincidence?"

Big John's face lit up with hope at last. "That's more like it, Brett. That's the sort of serious reasoning I expect you to come up with. We'll work on it. Were the other two killed in a way that's relevant to something in their lives?"

This time the Messenger had been more cautious. There were no witnesses and the scene-of-the-crime team had not found any promising leads. Brett, Clare and John took the latest calling card to add to Greta's chilling collection. On the way back to Sheffield, where they would add poison and spectacles to the growing list of the Messenger's weapons and keepsakes, they called in at Flint. Almost a month after the Messenger had strangled Leanne, John wanted to speak again to her devastated parents. They stood together in the hallway like coy, frightened creatures. They remembered John but had forgotten his name. If they could have plunged deeper into despair, they would have done so when they saw him filling their doorway. They stared blankly and mumbled, "Chief…"

"Superintendent Macfarlane," John said, finishing for them. "I'm sorry but I have to ask you something else."

In the suffocating atmosphere of the front room the parents sat despondently on the sofa and held each other by the hand, demonstrating that a murder always leaves more than one victim. The Messenger had taken their lives as well. He had destroyed their family.

"I ask you to keep this to yourselves," John said, "but we think whoever killed Leanne has killed again. There's something you can tell me that might stop him inflicting the same pain on someone else. OK?"

Leanne's mother murmured, "No matter what we say, she won't come back."

Squeezing his wife's hand, Leanne's dad nodded at John. "What is it?"

"This man, he might—"

"Man!" Leanne's mother cried out. "He's not a man. He's a monster!"

"True," John replied. "That's why we've got to catch him. He might be murdering his victims in particular ways. We think he drowned a swimmer, for instance. If that's right, it means he knows his victims, or he studies them before he kills. If it's true, it's very important to the investigation. It would help us enormously if we can decide whether he selects his victims carefully or just picks them at random. What do you think? I'm sorry, but I have to ask. Is there any reason he might have chosen to *strangle* Leanne?"

The wretched parents looked at each other vacantly. It was obvious that John's suggestion meant nothing to them.

Over John's shoulder, Clare put in, "Was she into singing, maybe?"

Leanne's mum was reduced to weeping silently but her father mumbled, "No. Nothing like that."

"All right," John said gently. He held out a card. "If you think of anything, give me a call. You can leave a message for me on that number."

In the car, Brett was unusually quiet. He was struck by the grief in Leanne's joyless home and he feared for her parents' future. Now that their young daughter had been taken from them, what did they have to look forward to? What would they feel? Bitterness, isolation, forgiveness, an overwhelming need for retribution? He could not imagine them forgiving the Messenger. A desire for retribution was much more likely, and Brett could not blame them for it.

It wasn't a particularly long journey but John couldn't survive it without a pie and a pint. They stopped at a pub and Brett offered to drive the rest of the way when Clare hinted that the bar sold one of her favourite ales. Brett and Clare didn't fancy anything from the food menu so, in a corner of the pub, they watched the chief consume his meal. While Big John swallowed pieces of pie like a whale engulfing plankton, Brett telephoned ahead. He wanted to know the background of the Uttoxeter victim.

By the time they got back to Sheffield, the Staffordshire police force had looked into the history of the woman who had been knifed in the tranquil grounds of a church. There was nothing in her past that suggested an affinity with knives. She wasn't even a regular church-goer. The new facts did not fit the theory of a connection between the victims' lifestyles and the manner of their deaths so Brett dismissed the idea. He said to John, "I'll take the calling card to Forensics. I still think analysis might hold the key and lead us to the Messenger."

John grunted, "We all know crimes are solved by detectives. Forensic evidence might suggest this or that – maybe even confirm it – but more often than not it's irrelevant or inaccurate. I'm going to call in a psychologist. The answer's up here," he said, pointing to the side of his head. "That's where we need to be – inside his brain."

11

While the psychologist studied the case notes on her own, John went with Brett and Clare to see Chief Inspector Smith of the Nottinghamshire Drug Squad, an oily, smug man with a plush office. "Ah," he said contemptuously. "So *you're* the ones."

John leaned heavily against a filing cabinet. "What about it?" he retorted, taking an instant dislike to the police officer.

"Do you know how close you came to ruining a major operation?"

"Are you saying the chap in the nightclub is one of yours?" Brett asked indignantly.

"Not as such," Smith reported evasively.

"Is he an undercover officer or not?" John demanded to know.

"Not quite. He's … helping us out."

"You mean," John hissed, translating Smith's cagey comments, "he's someone you got on a drugs charge but you did a deal with him rather than arrest him straightaway. In exchange for a sympathetic treatment of his case, he's mingling with the bad boys to pass information back to you."

"That's pretty close. And he's doing a good job, infiltrating the right circles. I'm banking on him to lead me to some big dealers. So," he snapped, "I won't have any further interference with him. Leave him alone."

Big John was quietly simmering. "His type's hardly trustworthy. Don't you think he might be using his work for you as a front for murder? While he enjoys your protection, maybe your snout thinks he's free to indulge himself in another pastime. Maybe he thinks he's untouchable because he's helping the Drug Squad. Let me tell you, he isn't."

"Oh?" Suddenly, Smith seemed perturbed, no longer in control.

"Here are the options," John stated. "One: we pull him in to question him – and risk his cover. Two: you pull on his leash and get us an interview."

"It's Tuesday," Brett put in. "If I'm not mistaken, we *could* grab him tonight. Doesn't he hang out at Mixers every Tuesday?"

Smith thumped his desk. "You can't jeopardize—"

"If you don't like either of those two options, there's number three. You provide us with exact details of his movements since Christmas Eve, up to and including yesterday. Especially yesterday," John stressed, thinking of the Oswestry murder. "And the information will have to be verified by the officer you'll have assigned to liaise with him – his handler."

"I don't see why you think you're more—"

"Look," John said. "We're after a serial killer, one with Ecstasy on his coat sleeve. And your man was seen dancing with one of our victims less than an hour before her head was cracked open. I think that takes precedence over your private arrangement with a dealer, don't you?"

"I'm not willing to take any action that'll endanger my case," Smith objected. "I'm close to some people who you don't want on the streets with your kids."

"And I'm after the most dangerous man in the land right now. It's the biggest case this country's seen in the last year or two. If anything holds it up, it could easily escalate into the biggest ever. To put it simply, I'm pulling rank. My inquiry *will* come first. You *will* get me an interview or the details I need." As much as John was capable of storming anywhere, he stormed out of the room.

Salma was a young consultant psychologist who called herself a behavioural investigator. Her services were not normally needed but, in particularly notorious cases, several police forces had called upon her expertise. While the forensic team searched a murder scene for minuscule bits of physical evidence to identify the culprit, Salma looked for shadowy and abstract evidence of his motivation – hatred, rage, fear, passion. In her last job for the police, after she'd examined the files of four murders committed by the same person, she'd proposed that the detectives should look for a white macho male in his thirties who would drive a flashy car, carry weapons and have trouble keeping a job. In her offender profile, she suggested that he'd be into pranks, teasing and torture, and that he'd have difficulties forming relationships with the opposite sex. When the police caught the perpetrator, he turned out to be white, divorced, the owner of a sports car, twenty-nine years of age, a bodybuilder, currently unemployed and on probation for assault. John had given her free access to all of the information on the Messenger's crimes.

She leaned back in the chair with her hands clasped behind her head. Spilled on the desk in front of her was the photographic record of the Messenger's seemingly senseless trade. "It's difficult – and possibly wrong – to classify a psychopathic personality as inborn or acquired during childhood," she pronounced. "Despite popular belief, it's not so much a mental problem as a moral defect. In other words, he's not mad. It's one extreme of human behaviour. Psychopaths have normal intelligence – often well above normal – but never grow out of a childlike selfishness. Your man's immature. He doesn't have conventional emotional responses and he has no conscience at all. He hasn't acquired the blocks that stop the rest of us from just taking what we want, from thumping or killing anyone in our way. He'll have whims and if he doesn't get his way, he'll resort to aggression like a frustrated kid. Any challenge to his self-esteem will be met with extreme violence. It's the only way he knows so he won't feel any regret or remorse whatsoever. To him, other people are unimportant. If they stop him from gratifying himself, he'll brush them aside. Now brushing them aside's become his form of gratification. He's all the more dangerous *because* he doesn't have a mental disorder. He can plan his violence cleverly and efficiently. He's a classic case. Your Messenger's become a power and control serial killer.

"He feels he's got no control over his own life so he seeks control over others – over *their* lives and deaths. The crime scenes show he was in command and that's how he'd like it. But, unlike some, there's no sign of violence to the victim before he despatches them. That's unusual. Also, power and control killers tend to kill somewhere secluded – often their own homes, sometimes their victims' – and then dump the bodies where they'll be found, mostly by roads. Your Messenger's slightly different: he goes straight for the roadside. Of course, his messages are important to him so he wouldn't want to conceal his victims. He wants them to be found pretty quickly, complete with calling card."

"He left one victim in her own home, and one in his own garage," Brett interjected.

"Yes," Salma responded thoughtfully. "I'm not sure about that, but I said he's a bit different. Perhaps he knew someone was about to call and would discover the bodies. Perhaps he's just... No, I'll save that for later," she decided. "For the moment, let's think about his victims. He probably preys on them at random, whoever's convenient, approaching them to ask for help or offering to give help. In the eighties a serial killer in the States put a false plaster cast on his arm and then went up to his victims asking for help with something. When the police got him, his room was awash with plaster of Paris and gauze. Before he was executed he admitted killing thirty-six women but his real tally was thought to be over three hundred. Anyway, your Messenger and his messages. They prove he's not in command of his otherwise anonymous life. He's determined to make it big by being dramatic. He wants fame. He thinks exerting his power over others will do the trick. He can't wait to get reported on the news – that would spur him on even more. I suggest you do all you can to keep a lid on this one. Of course, he wants to get caught as well. That's the ultimate fame – when everyone'll know him. But not yet. He's got some plan and it's not finished yet, no matter what his last message says. He'll keep changing his methods and his victims till he's completed his plan – or until he gets caught."

Big John sat on the other side of the desk, nodding encouragingly now and again. Brett wanted to push

Salma on. He was impatient for specific detail. John was happy to absorb and wait. Except when he was provoked or in a bad mood, he had infinite patience. That's how he got the best out of people – by giving them time to do it their way.

"It's a sure characteristic for this type of murderer to take a remembrance – a trophy – away from each murder," Salma disclosed, "even if it means mutilating the victim's body. Gruesome, you might think, but perfectly logical and legitimate to him. You see, in his self-centred world, he can do what he wants with those he's overpowered. The Messenger's not entirely typical, I know, but I think he'll show quite a few of the other classic traits. He'll be fairly skilled, for example, but possibly an underachiever. He'll blame everyone but himself for that. Generally, black serial killers kill blacks and white ones kill whites. So, your man's almost certainly white. I'm not sure about age but he might have a cosy traditional marriage, possibly with children. If he does, he'll rule over a timid wife and kids like a tyrant. But that bit of control wouldn't be enough for him. It wouldn't bring him national recognition. He probably suffered inconsistent discipline himself as a child. You know, at one moment spoiled and the next given a thorough thrashing. Perhaps one of his parents would be absent for long stretches. Quite possibly, it wasn't a caring environment for a youngster. Psychopaths aren't born bad – family dysfunction makes them, not genetics. Anyway, in their everyday lives, power and control killers often have peculiarities that set them apart and make them unpopular: speech defects, antisocial behaviour, rampant acne, that sort of thing." She paused before emphasizing, "And he'll have shown an interest in the case. I bet you already know him. He'll be in your file somewhere. Maybe he reported finding one of the bodies or thrust himself forward as a witness, but he'll have surfaced somewhere. He's playing with you. That's almost certainly the reason for his frequent changes of MO, including the woman in her own bathroom. He's taunting you. Especially you, Brett. It'd be no fun if he didn't see his enemy close up. I think you'll have his name already."

Brett was sceptical about offender profiling. To him, the results were too general, woolly and quite likely to be wrong because they were based on opinion and statistical probabilities rather than hard evidence. Even so, he was intrigued by Salma's references to parental discipline, speech defects and spots. He had to admit, "At times, you could've been describing one of our suspects, Ian Lowe, perfectly."

Butting in, John murmured, "Pity we can't bring him in on a charge of possession of an offensive stammer or a serious case of acne."

"Yes, but he's not married."

"I don't claim one hundred per cent accuracy," Salma put in. "I deal with likelihood. I've been wrong in the past – and I've hit quite a few nails squarely on the head. I'll tell you this, though, I'm confident that I'm at least fifty per cent right."

"Yeah, but which fifty per cent?" Brett replied.

By way of explaining Brett's attitude, John chipped in derogatorily, "He's the scientific sort."

"Ah. Well, you'll think of me as a soft scientist then, but I use the same rigour as any other scientist. It's just that human behaviour is a complex subject. It's influenced by a huge number of interacting factors: biology, culture, childhood experiences, education, environment and a million other things. Physical scientists deal with simpler systems that they can control more precisely, that's all. Let me put it this way: do you believe forensic results are always right?" Salma said with a cheeky grin.

"Always, yes," Brett replied. "We might misinterpret the results, though. And someone might've done a bad experiment so we get an answer to the wrong question. But the results are right even if we humans sometimes foul it up."

"OK," Salma rejoined, "but you'll be familiar with experimental uncertainty. Any result has uncertainty – science or psychology. My findings have a wider degree of uncertainty than most scientific studies, that's all. Think of my description as a target. The bull's-eye's on it somewhere, now it's up to you to hit it."

Weary and frustrated by the pace of the investigation, Brett and Clare left the police station at the same time. To block out unsavoury images, they chatted about anything but murder. In the cold night air, their breath formed speech bubbles for frivolous words. They decided to drive to Clare's favourite pub and fish restaurant in Hathersage, where they would drown their conceptions of the Messenger in real ale. She would enjoy swordfish steak or red snapper and he would grumble melodramatically about her limitless appetite for his favourite creatures and order a vegetarian dish.

Their plans for a pleasant evening of utter trivia were ambushed even before they reached the car park. They were stopped in their tracks by a question shouted at Brett by a reporter with a small notebook. "Has Macfarlane been brought in because *you're* not getting anywhere, Inspector Lawless?"

Stung by the insult, Brett's first impulse was to deny the slur on his competence but he thought before he spoke. He could not answer the criticism without revealing the widened scope of the investigation, and there was a news blackout on the case. Publicity was what the Messenger wanted and what Brett could least afford to give. A seasoned officer would have ignored the question altogether or simply snorted, "No comment." Brett was more civil. He stopped walking, hesitated, and then replied, "The fact that Detective Chief Superintendent Macfarlane is on the case simply reflects the importance we attach to finding Nicola Morrison's killer. That's all."

"Has he been put in charge because of the other murders, then?"

Clare was stunned into silence. Brett opened his

mouth but then shut it again. It was not a time for more politeness. "Which paper are you from?" he barked.

"Local. *The Sheffield Gazette.*"

"What are these other murders you're talking about?"

"Cambridge and Flint, for example. That's what we were reliably told. Where were you today, Inspector Lawless?"

"No comment at all," Brett turned and walked back towards the station.

Clare followed him, muttering, "A leak! John's not going to like it."

"It's worse than that," Brett replied in a whisper. "Do you believe any of the team talked to the press?"

"No, not on a case like this."

"In questioning," Brett muttered, "we've asked suspects about Cheltenham and North Wales but we've never mentioned Flint to them."

"So, no one knows about Flint," said Clare.

"Well, *one* person does, and he's not batting for our team," Brett declared ominously.

It was like watching a volcano erupt. Even the hardened editor of *The Sheffield Gazette* was taken aback and wished that he had not decided to uphold the principle of never revealing his sources.

"There are only two ways you could have found out about my inquiry," Big John boomed. "From one of my officers or from the culprit. Now, I trust my officers' discretion so I assume you've got the story from the killer." He peered angrily into the editor's face and added, "Given that, don't you think you have a duty to tell me your source?"

This wasn't the John Macfarlane with unending patience. This was John Macfarlane reacting to an unnecessary obstacle. Brett watched the spectacle.

"That's as may be, but a newspaper has to protect—"

"And I have to protect the public from a killer without a conscience," John snarled. "Don't tell me you haven't got one either. If he strikes again while you're sitting on vital information, your conscience'll never let you sleep again. And the public won't exactly thank you for putting the interests of a psychopath and a scoop before theirs."

The editor sighed. Reluctantly, he muttered, "It was a phone call."

"Surprise, surprise!" John hissed sarcastically. "No record of it – unless you taped it."

"No, I just listened."

"A male voice?"

"Not the deepest male voice I've ever heard but, yes, male. Muffled as well. I think he was disguising it somehow. The accent shifted and he only spoke for a few seconds. Before you ask, I couldn't get a fix on his age or where he comes from."

"Weren't you suspicious about this character? Why didn't you call us?" asked Brett.

The editor shrugged. "I thought he might've been a police officer, trying to earn a bit of cash on the side by breaking an embargo of some sort."

Brett frowned. "If money was his game, if he was selling a story, don't you think he'd be talking to the big boys with the big cheque books? *News of the World* or something."

"Perhaps he did. He didn't say he was offering an exclusive."

"What *did* he say?" Clare enquired.

"Not a lot – it was a very short call. He just said it wasn't only Nicola Morrison. He said we ought to look into other murders in Cheltenham, Flint, Cambridge and Uttoxeter. That's it. No details. We put a man on it – as you know – to find out if there was anything in it, such as it was. Looks like we touched a nerve. By coming here, you've confirmed it."

"Well, you can forget the story," John decided. Dabbing his forehead with a crumpled handkerchief, he uttered, "Drop it. I know this type of killer – publicity's exactly what he wants. If he gets some, he'll want more. He'll feed on it and grow. You wouldn't want any responsibility for his future deeds, would you?" The question was delivered like a statement.

"Drop it? No chance! Not when several of the nationals'll be on to it as well, if I'm any judge. If this man's after publicity, he won't stop with us. No point turning off one tap when there's a deluge coming."

"It wouldn't be the first time all newspapers have agreed to keep a lid on something for the sake of public safety," John noted.

"Not in a case like this," the editor retorted. "You're thinking of kidnap cases. We've volunteered to keep quiet when we've been assured by you lot that breaking the story could put a specific hostage at greater risk. That's different – the crime's already happening and someone's in danger. We'll cooperate then. Here, the threat's not against an individual, it's general. I'd argue that it's in the public's interest to alert everyone to it *before* he strikes again. That way, I'm providing a service because people can protect themselves by staying behind locked doors if they want to. There *will* be a story, Chief Superintendent."

"Then you may well encourage him. I hope you'll feel proud of yourself," John said caustically.

"I'll feel proud of informing people about a danger. That's my job. I couldn't encourage him at all if you did yours and caught him."

John groaned. "Your intervention won't make the job any easier."

"I'll tell you something that might, then," the editor added. "If it was your culprit I spoke to, perhaps you can make sense of this. Before he rang off, he said, 'I've got to go now – to the top of a...' something. I didn't catch the last word."

"The last word – the one you missed – was probably the only significant one," John grunted.

"He's into playing games," Clare observed. "Perhaps you weren't meant to hear it."

"Can I quote you on that?"

"No," John exclaimed. "Don't push your luck!"

On Wednesday morning, Liz was impatient to convey her latest findings. When she burned with excitement, it usually meant she had something significant or outlandish, or both. "First," she announced, "the bread-and-butter stuff that's come in. Lance Golby's trip to Telford checked out. He did a job there. He also had enough free time to pop up to Oswestry at the time of the murder. Purcell claims he went fishing for the day but he can't give us any witnesses. Ian Lowe – he's plain lying. Says he was at home. When I said I'd been calling him, he stammered something about not wanting to answer the phone."

"What else, Liz?" asked Clare. "You're itching to give us something."

"The Oswestry calling card. It took Greta a while to identify the writing, but she has." After a tantalizing pause, she told them, "Apparently, it comes from *Our Dogs*."

"*Our Dogs!*" John growled. "Never heard of it."

With a flourish, Liz produced a copy of the paper. "I went out and bought one. Riveting. 'Over a century of canine publishing' it says on the front cover."

"OK, Brett," John said mischievously, "you think the papers are significant. Let's hear your theory about *Our Dogs*."

Brett could do nothing but shrug and smile sadly. "Beats me." He didn't have a theory but he had a feeling that he'd seen a similar magazine before.

"There's something else," Liz put in, grinning. "I had a call from a WPC Jenson in Notts. Said she wanted to leave a message for you, Brett. A resourceful young recruit, it seems – keen cookie. In her spare time, she's done a bit of research on Anna Stimpson, the theatrical agent. She's not exactly full of confidence, this Louise Jenson. She insisted I check out her information before passing it on. She was right, though. Many years ago, our Miss Stimpson was on the stage herself. It didn't work out so she started her agency instead."

"All right, Liz," Brett said. "Give us the punch-line. What did she do?"

"A number of things, but the highlight of her performance was song and dance in drag. She was a male impersonator."

It was a difficult interview. Continual interruptions from the telephone, the bleeps of incoming urgent E-mail, and an uncooperative Anna Stimpson. "I don't know how I can help you further, Inspector Lawless. I told you I found the car and that's all. I'm beginning to wish I hadn't been so public-spirited and reported it."

"We're sorry to have to bother you again, but other matters have since come to light and we have to retrace our steps a bit. Routine inquiries, you could say," Brett replied cagily.

"All right," Anna murmured begrudgingly. "Let's get on with it."

He glanced round her office and smiled at all of the pictures on her walls – prints of playhouses, stills from Shakespeare plays, snapshots of song and dance routines, scenes from soaps, portraits, comedians and clowns. Even two glossy photographs of her dogs. "You came here – to your office – on the morning of the eighteenth, but you must have to travel a lot in this business. Seeing clients, producers, plays and the like."

"True."

"So," Brett asked directly, "where do you go to, typically?"

"All the significant cities – London, Manchester, Stratford, Bristol, Swansea, Edinburgh. Plenty of others, but I guess they're the main ones."

"How about Christmas Eve?"

Anna's eyes narrowed as she cast a withering look at Brett. "What's this? An accusation?"

Making light of it, Brett smiled. "Not at all. Routine inquiries, as I said. We need to know where you were on Christmas Eve and New Year's Day. At the beginning of this week as well – Monday – and, while we're at it, last Thursday if you can remember."

Indignant, Anna snarled, "As it turns out, I *did* go to a play – a Christmas Eve special in Bristol, where one of my actors landed the role of Jesus. I was at home on New Year's Day and I was here in the office last week, Monday as well. Is that enough?"

"Not quite," Brett replied. "Is there anyone who could back you up? Someone who saw you at home or here?"

"When I reported that broken-down car, I didn't expect this sort of hassle. Next time, I'll look the other way."

"It's unfortunate," Clare interjected, "but can you answer the question, please? It *is* vital information."

"I've done nothing, Sergeant Tilley, except report a disabled car. And, no, I live on my own. I relish my privacy. No one can vouch for me when I'm at home. Several people would've phoned me here on Monday, and last Thursday but I'd have trouble remembering those."

While Clare took down the details of her Monday callers, Brett pretended to examine the displays on the wall behind her. When Anna had stopped dictating names and telephone numbers, Brett said, "Is that you? In that photo," he said, pointing over her shoulder.

Anna's eyebrows rose. "You're very observant. It was taken a long time ago and I'm buried under quite a layer of make-up but, yes, it's me."

She was wearing a man's dark suit, a flamboyant shirt and a contrasting blue tie. A bowler hat was perched on her head. In one hand, she was twirling a cane and in the other she held a microphone. Pleasantly, Brett said, "You made a good man."

"Not good enough. It didn't last."

"Did you attempt to sing as a man as well?" Brett asked. "You know – deep voice. Or was it part of the fun to sing like a woman while dressed as a man?"

Becoming suspicious that Brett was not indulging in small talk, she answered tersely, "I acted the part of a man. The whole hog."

"Pity it didn't take off," Brett said.

"I'm quite satisfied doing my present job. I might have been drawn to fame once but not so much now.

There's value in being anonymous. I see the problems my actors face: they loathe not working and then they loathe fame – being recognized everywhere they go, the press snapping every indiscretion. They can't win. Some can't handle it."

"Interesting," Clare replied. "I don't want to pry..." Ignoring Anna's sharp stare, she continued, "but I guess some of them might get involved in drugs. To escape the problems for a while."

"It's not unheard of," Anna responded warily.

"Have you come into contact with drugs or drug users?"

"Not knowingly," she answered.

Brett stood up and said, "Thanks. Just one last thing. You take the magazine *Our Dogs*, don't you?"

Exasperated again, Anna was almost lost for words. "I don't know what you're getting at!" she spluttered. "Yes, I do take it."

"Strange question, I know," Brett admitted, "but necessary. Thanks for being so patient. That's all for now."

Sometimes, Brett did not like what he had to do. If Anna Stimpson was a perfectly innocent theatrical agent, he had just upset and insulted her. But, he had to remind himself, if she was a good actress with a grudge against the world for snubbing her performances, he had treated her lightly. He regretted that he often had to assume anyone could be guilty.

On the way to the car, Clare said, "It's strange how many people hanker after fame, isn't it? Like the

131

Messenger. Especially if they've tasted it once. Terry Purcell and now Anna Stimpson."

"You didn't believe her then?"

"She didn't say she didn't want fame," Clare pointed out. "She said she didn't want it as much as she used to. That still leaves a lot of scope. She could be a wolf in sheep's clothing. She could be our man, making a crisis out of her drama."

Clare slapped her techno-junkie colleague on the shoulder. "More riveting police work for you, Liz."

"Oh, yeah?" she responded cynically.

"A whole load of phone numbers. Anna Stimpson says these people called her on her Sheffield office number on Monday. If they did, she's off the hook. Fancy splitting the job? Fifty-fifty."

"All right," she grumbled. "I think I can stand the excitement."

Brett added, "Can you do something for me as well? Find out if any one football team played within striking distance of each of our murders? Include the day before and the day after the killing, just to make sure. A travelling fan could've stopped overnight."

"Typical man," Liz observed. "Suffering from football fixation."

"Papers!" someone boomed across the incident room. "And you ain't going to like it."

The Messenger's public reign of terror had begun. The investigative journalists had not wasted time. Several papers had discovered and reported three of the murders. The prize went to the *Guardian* with five of the Messenger's six misdeeds. Luckily, none of the reporters had discovered the more macabre aspects of the murders. The messages and the mementoes were not mentioned. Using Brett's press release but misquoting him, the article in *The Sun* ended, *The police said there's a chance he might try it again. He has. It's time to get hysterical.* The phrase had come back to haunt Brett.

13

Greg bellowed across the chaotic incident room, "I've got a medium – a psychic – on the line. Says she's seen the papers and she's receiving vibes or something from the Messenger. Thinks she can help us find him. Do we want to speak to her?"

Simultaneously, Brett shouted, "No!" and John answered, "Yes."

With his hand still over the mouthpiece, Greg looked from one to the other.

"You go and see her, Greg," Big John decided. "Find out if she's a crank or not. We need every bit of help we can get on this one. But make sure no reporters follow you – I don't want *Police consult fortune-teller* splattered all over *The Mirror* tomorrow."

Slowly the clamour of the day subsided. Officers

departed to explore leads, returned from dead-ends, or went off duty. The optimism and energy of a team pursuing one strong lead was missing. The investigation was like a rudderless ship, drifting with the prevailing current. A new idea and the team followed it slavishly, only to be driven back on the next tide. If the Messenger knew that they were all at sea, he would be laughing even louder.

Eventually, late at night, Brett was left on his own like a captain refusing to desert his craft. Rain hammered frantically on the roof as he sipped hot coffee that tasted as synthetic as the polystyrene cup. He gazed again at the map with its depressing trail of drawing pins that marked the Messenger's catalogue of cruelty.

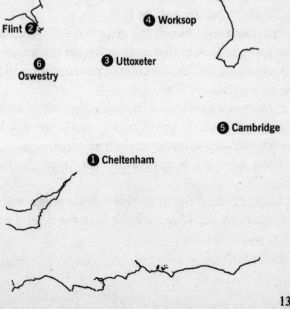

Everything that Brett had been taught told him that there would be a link between the Messenger's separate crimes, but he couldn't see it. He didn't even know where to look for the link. Was it the victims, the messages, the locations, the dates, the keepsakes? The map didn't reveal anything to him. It was as baffling and infuriating as his Magic Eye picture.

When the door opened, Brett turned in surprise.

"I thought I'd find you in here," his partner said. "They don't pay you for overtime, you know." Clare's red hair was wet and flat against her head and she looked tired.

"Been running through the rain?"

Clare smiled. "No. Working out in the gym. Finished with a shower."

"You must be feeling better after your cold."

"Yeah. What are you up to?"

Brett nodded towards the map. "One of these days, I'm going to look at that map, or his list of victims, or his messages, or his collection of mementoes, and see the connection. It'll be obvious."

"Then you won't see it by sitting here till midnight, trying too hard. If you're right, you'll see it when you're least expecting it – a flash of inspiration."

Brett let out a long breath. "You might be right but—"

Clare finished for him. "How many more will he get before we see what's staring us in the face? That's what you're thinking."

Brett nodded.

Clare got herself a coffee from the machine and joined him. "What do you think about this Friday? He was due to strike again on the second of February. Will he?"

Brett shrugged. "Who knows? Possibly. Or maybe Michael Black on Monday satisfied him for this week." He sighed. "How did you and Liz get on with those phone calls to Anna Stimpson's clients?"

"Still checking. Some of them are tricky to find – off doing shows. We've got a few who remember calling her at her office on Monday, though."

"So she's…" Brett hesitated before ruling her out. "What time of day did they call?"

Clare grinned. "Good to see you're still on the ball at this time of night. So far, they say they phoned in the afternoon or evening. Michael Black was murdered in the morning. She's not in the clear yet. In the morning she could've been driving back from Oswestry."

Brett turned to the dormant computer and typed a brief E-mail message for Greta in Forensics: *Any trace of theatrical make-up or dog hairs (Dobermann pinscher) at any of the Messenger's crime scenes?* He looked at Clare and asked, "Imagine it *is* Anna Stimpson. What difference would you see between a man, and a woman pretending to be a man?"

Clare inhaled deeply. "I don't know … except…"

"What?"

She could not keep a grin from her face as she replied, "Which loo she'd use."

"What did the crystal ball show you?" John enquired when, on Thursday, Greg returned from his visit to the medium in Rotherham.

"She claimed she could read his troubled spirit."

"Oh, yeah?" Brett murmured.

"She was genuine," Greg said. "*She* believed it. Trying to help in her own sweet way, but decidedly batty. She hadn't really got anything, but ... she said he must be quite close for her to feel his presence so strongly. And, er, she felt certain the Messenger was not all he seemed to be. Quite insistent on that, she was. She talked about him living a lie."

Clare put in, "Like Brett, I don't go for this psychic stuff – because I can't understand it – but she could be describing Anna Stimpson. She certainly isn't what she seems to be if she goes on the prowl as a man."

Brett dismissed the medium's opinions. To him, it seemed that consulting someone claiming to be clairvoyant was scraping the bottom of the barrel. Beyond that, behavioural profiling was more respectable, but both fell far short of physical evidence.

Later in the day, Liz called out, "No football-fan connection, Brett. No one team's been near all our locations at the right time."

"So we can't even nail a Manchester United fan," Clare joked. "Pity!"

"Thanks, anyway," Brett said. "Update on the Anna Stimpson phone calls?"

"Yeah," Liz answered. "All those people *did* phone, but your starlet forgot to tell you something: the earliest call was at two-fifteen in the afternoon. I think actors sleep till lunch. Gives their agent time to go out on a killing spree first."

Clare chipped in, "And we've been asking if any of them called her last Thursday as well. Those that could remember that far back said they didn't."

"Anne the man's still in the frame," Liz concluded.

Throughout the day, the tension mounted. No one voiced their worries about the next day and what it might bring, but it was in everyone's mind. Privately, they could see the Messenger, wearing the easy unnerving smile of the complete psychotic, choosing newspapers and magazines, cutting out letters and words as if they were the hearts of his victims, planning his next kill, his next message. His erratic shift of schedule had caused an oppressive uncertainty. Somehow, the pressure would have been more bearable if they'd known for sure that he would kill again on Friday. He'd become ominously unpredictable.

"That editor said the Messenger made a last remark on the phone. What was it?" Answering his own question, Brett murmured, " 'I've got to go now – to the top of a…' Then he stopped. Let's have that up on the wall with the rest of his literary output, just in case it meant something. I bet it wasn't idle chatter."

He printed the words on a piece of paper and fixed it to the wall under his other messages.

I am somebody.
She will help me
make a name for myself.
You will be getting to know me.
Lawless on TV. Soon it will be me.
I am complete.
I've got to go now – to the top of a...

Brett stared at the list of sayings and shook his head. He mumbled, "I wish we'd got that last word – or words."

Brett's request for more forensic information did not advance the case. Greta found traces of make-up on some objects from the murder scenes but in each case they matched that worn by the victim. Dog hairs had been found on three separate items. The old lady in Cheltenham owned a poodle and its moulted fur clung to her clothing. Two dog hairs had turned up on Peter Colburn's jacket but they had come from Terry Purcell's dogs on the Cambridge golf course. The hairs could have been transferred directly from the dogs if they had brushed against the body while they sniffed at it, or indirectly from Terry Purcell's hands or clothing. The third object contaminated with dog fur was the bloodstained and abandoned coat. Greta might have found it simpler to list what she hadn't detected on Bill's discovery. It had come into contact with all sorts: hair from humans, cats, Alsatians, Dobermanns, mongrels, rats. Along with the Ecstasy, there were traces of newspaper print, meat, cigarettes, crisps, mud, soot — just about everything. Of course, it was impossible to tell which residues were a result of Bill's lifestyle and which originated from its previous owner. As evidence it was useless, but there *were* Dobermann hairs on it.

"Tomorrow, let's put a couple of officers on Anna Stimpson, Ian Lowe, Lance Golby and the out-of-catchment suspects like Terry Purcell," Brett suggested.

"If we put one car on each of them, they'll know they're being followed as soon as they start to move," John said, belittling Brett's suggestion. "And we don't have enough troops to tail that many people seriously — so that they don't know they're under surveillance. We'd need about forty cars and over a hundred people for a proper job. And we'd have to set up at least five different control centres."

"I know," Brett replied, "but only one of them can be the Messenger — at most. Sure, it'd be easy for that one to spot the surveillance and shake it off, but if he — or she — *does* strike tomorrow, we might eliminate one, two, maybe more of the others because they might stay at home or be miles from the murder. I doubt if we'd lose *all* the others."

Big John relented. "OK, you've got a point. You organize it. But if the Messenger's among our suspects, he'll spot our officers and stay at home himself. That's my guess. No murder. A waste."

Clare interjected, "If it stops him murdering tomorrow, I wouldn't say it's a waste."

John Macfarlane nodded. "That's not what I meant. A waste because we're no closer. And we can't keep a watch for ever. We can't tie up that many officers indefinitely on such a long shot. We can't even predict his hit days any more, so we can't concentrate surveillance efforts at the right time."

"E-mail!" Liz chirped. "You've been invited out for a pint with a Sergeant Alan Rennie of the Notts drug barons tonight. He says he's willing to come over here to Sheffield. Eight-thirty in the Rose and Crown."

"Rose and Crown!" John exclaimed with disdain. "Typical Drug Squad – no taste."

"Warm gassy beer, darts and mushy peas," Clare commented.

"Oh, well," John said to her, "at least they got one thing right: mushy peas." To Liz, he said, "Tell him we'll be there. The drinks'll be on him."

Brett didn't need an introduction to recognize a fellow police officer. Just as a dog recognizes another dog by sight, no matter what the breed, so Brett recognized Alan Rennie. He was sitting on his own behind a pint of beer in the corner of the smoky bar. Yellowed foam was bursting through the cheap red plastic covering of the seat. The off-white paint on the ceiling and the upper half of the walls was far more off-white than it should have been. Over the years, smokers had tainted the walls and their own lungs at the same time, and Sergeant Rennie was continuing the process. It was odd, Brett thought, that those closest to the illicit drugs trade seemed to have the highest intake of legalized ones.

John collected three drinks and a disgusting concoction of double chips, green lumpy sludge and a pasty before he joined Alan Rennie. Glancing round, John murmured quietly, "Are you going to produce this snout for us?"

"Sorry," Alan responded, shaking his head. "Too risky to be seen with police officers."

"What have you got, then?" asked John, tucking into his meal. "A confession?"

Alan smiled. "A knowledge of his movements," he replied, pulling a logbook from his coat pocket.

"First things first," John said. "What's his name?"

"Dundee. Everyone calls him Croc – you know, Crocodile Dundee – but his real name's Stuart."

"A mole called Crocodile!" John grunted with both derision and humour. "OK, give us his whereabouts. Brett'll tell you which days while I…" He illustrated his intentions by pointing at his food and then shovelling some chips into his mouth.

"You spoke to him about his movements, did you?" Brett enquired. "You can verify them?"

Alan shrugged. "Some, yes. Not all. Let's hope I can assure you about at least some of the days that are important to you."

Wiping his mouth and trying to avoid spitting any food across the table, John put in, "Now, as his handler, you wouldn't be thinking of providing your man with alibis just to get us off his back, would you?"

Alan looked offended. "No. I understand you've got a major inquiry – it's all over every newspaper in the land."

"You're handling this Croc so you'll know him," Clare reasoned. "How dangerous is he?"

"Very dangerous to some dealers, because he's got evidence against them. We've just got to reel him in at the right time so he can shop as many of them as possible. We leave him out long enough to get lots of evidence against the big boys but not long enough for them to suss him out."

"I meant, is he a killer or just a dealer in death?" Clare prompted in a hushed voice.

"It's a rough world. He's not the sort that kills for fun like yours, though. Until he started to work with us, he might've gone to extremes to protect his business. Now he'd protect himself, but that's about it, I think."

"OK, down to dates," Brett said. "Christmas Eve first."

Alan glanced at his notes and admitted, "Nothing confirmed. Could've been anywhere." With a cigarette perched in the corner of his mouth, he slurred his words. "Claimed to be at home in Worksop."

"Monday, New Year's Day."

"Ditto."

"How about the ninth of January? Tuesday."

"I saw him that morning. We've got a secure meeting place in Mansfield. I had to warn him about a raid we were planning on Mixers. We only did it because the dealers get suspicious if they don't see any evidence of activity. Without a bit of action, they might think we're planning something more under-hand, so we gave them a raid to make them think we're still fishing in the dark. I warned Croc so he didn't get caught up in it."

"Does he go to Mixers every Tuesday? We know he was there on the sixteenth and twenty-third."

"Uh-huh," Alan confirmed as he dragged at his cigarette.

"Thursday the twenty-fifth."

Alan scanned his log again. "He had a meeting in London." Lowering his voice again, he added, "Picked up a little something."

"How did he go? Car?"

"Yes."

"So he could've dropped in on Cambridge."

"Suppose so," Alan murmured, stubbing out his cigarette.

"This Monday," Brett said, giving his last date.

"No problem. East Anglia. There from Sunday till Tuesday morning. Some unpatrolled bit of shoreline. He met a couple of boats from Holland. It's the in-place to drop off incoming drugs from Europe – lots of isolated beaches and safe places for speedboats to land."

"You know this for certain?" Big John put in.

"Absolutely. I was nearby."

"Lurking in the sand dunes?"

"Not that close but, take my word for it, that's where he was."

The end of the line. Croc, the unknown disco dancer, was in the clear. He couldn't be in East Anglia and Wales at the same time, and his witness was a police officer. There could hardly be a more watertight alibi. "Thanks," John said to Alan. "Good to see such willing cooperation across different forces and squads."

"You're dropping the idea of speaking to him directly?" Alan checked. It was almost a demand.

"He's off our wanted list," Brett assured Sergeant Rennie.

"Bit of advice about your Crocodile," Big John said as he stood. "Don't leave him out in the wild too long. His former colleagues will turn him into handbags if they find out what you're up to. We're too busy to investigate another killing."

The second day of February passed without a murder. John made sure that all police forces were on heightened alert. There were plenty of minor skirmishes, but no serious attempts on a life. Ian Lowe stayed at home, Terry Purcell went to his sports club and Anna Stimpson worked long hours in her Sheffield office. The Gloucestershire suspect bullied his nervy wife and terrorized his children over breakfast and then stormed out of the house. Like Lance Golby, he took to the road. Both of them eluded the officers who were tailing them. Brett's strategy came to nothing.

The next few days were also free of the Messenger's handiwork but his cloud still hung over England and Wales. In Coventry, a woman ran screaming from a stranger who only wanted to ask for directions to the railway station. A fourteen-year-old mugger in Liverpool was quizzed for hours by detectives, just in case. A nervous and overexcited crowd beat up a man who tried to force his way into a young woman's house. By the time the police arrived, he had been severely injured. But he wasn't the Messenger either – he was a debt-collector. The whole nation seemed to be on edge.

"It's gone quiet. Maybe he's basking in his new-found fame before he – or she – creates more mayhem," Greg ventured.

"Maybe he really has stopped, like his last message said," Liz suggested.

"Do you believe that?" asked Clare.

"No. He's addicted to killing."

"Exactly. He'll be back."

Yet the tenth of February – the next date in his original sequence – slipped by without a hint of murder. The lull did not last long, though.

14

It was Monday 12th February. On the way home from school on the outskirts of Macclesfield, Jayne's older sisters talked about grown-up things. Jayne was excluded and she lagged behind. Occasionally her sisters would turn and call out impatiently, "*Do* keep up, Jayne!" but they didn't wait. Jayne trotted after them but soon slowed to a dawdle again. There was so much to explore, so much to distract her. A dead sparrow under a tree. A ginger cat that sat on a garden wall pushed its head into her outstretched hand and purred loudly. A spider crawling into a discarded Pepsi can. A helicopter whirling noisily overhead. The sudden opening of a car door and a big hand reaching, grasping.

The journey to Macclesfield was not a happy one.

John was seething because the Messenger had sunk to new depths. Selecting a six-year-old victim showed that he was even more cowardly and heartless than John had thought. Brett was lost in frustration. The meagre pieces of reliable evidence were so flimsy that he could not get a firm grip on the identity or motivation of the killer. And he did not relish meeting another family destroyed by the Messenger. In the driving seat, Clare felt indignant and shocked by the Messenger's latest crime but she tried to remain detached. She knew that she would be more capable of tracking him down if she did not see him as he would be portrayed in the press – the personification of evil. Inside the car there was mostly a dismal and thoughtful silence. Outside it was just as dismal. The cloud cover was unerringly grey and a dreary mist hung in the air, draping the world in chiffon. Not even the beautiful Winnats Pass over the Peaks could lift the depression. By the time they reached Macclesfield, the sky had darkened to surly black. It seemed to suit their miserable task.

The tent was well lit and, from outside, two ominous silhouettes could be seen shifting uneasily within. John introduced himself, Brett and Clare to the officers on duty and then stepped into the temporary mausoleum near the golf course. When he saw the small bloodied victim, he allowed himself to snort with disgust and swear aloud before he resumed his normal dispassionate behaviour. Addressing the pathologist, he enquired, "What have we got, then?"

Brett looked at the body of the young girl, frowned and murmured, "Gemma."

The pathologist, about to answer Big John, hesitated. Puzzled, he glanced up at Brett and said, "No. Her name's Jayne."

John stared at Brett and uttered, "Gemma? Who's Gemma?"

In a daze, Brett mumbled, "Sorry. I don't know who Gemma... I just thought... Never mind. I'm, er, going to get some fresh air. Sorry."

After he'd gone, John grimaced at Clare, saying, "He flipped his lid once before when he saw a kid's body, you know. In that first case in Edale. Very unprofessional."

Defending her partner, Clare said, "I think he's feeling under the weather, that's all." She glanced at John and added, "If you can manage here, I'll just go and check if he's all right."

"I can manage," John grumbled. "The victim's not going anywhere."

Brett was leaning against the car, breathing deeply and gazing into the furious stained sky. Clare touched his sleeve and asked, "Are you OK, Brett?"

Without looking at her, he muttered, "Yes. I just don't know how anyone could..." He paused and looked into Clare's concerned face. She deserved more than a superficial response. She deserved the truth. "No," he admitted, "I feel pretty awful, actually. Dizzy. I feel as if I've seen all this before. Do you remember the baby at Upper Needless? I felt the same then. Before *that*, I don't really know. But something's nagging at me, telling me there was a girl called Gemma."

Clare tightened her grip on his arm. "What are you saying, Brett? What is this?"

"I'm not sure," he replied. "I think I'm going to contact Liz. I'll be OK. You'd better go back and hold the Chief's hand."

Clare was not at all convinced that he was well but she left him because that was what he wanted.

Brett slipped into the car and used the radiophone. "Liz," he said, doing his best to sound normal and composed, "I want you to check something for me. Registry of deaths. Can you do that?"

"Yeah," her voice replied. "I'm on-line. What name is it?"

Brett hesitated and then, with determination, answered, "Lawless."

"Lawless?" Liz exclaimed. "Is this part of the case, a joke or ... something else?"

"Just check, can you?"

"All right, Brett. When? And first name?"

"Gemma," he said into the radio. "I don't know the date. Let's say twenty to twenty-five years ago."

"Searching," Liz reported.

While he waited, Brett trembled and watched the heavy clouds drift like giant ugly ink blots across the moon.

He jumped when Liz's crackling disembodied

voice filled the car. "It's here," she said gingerly. Not her normal forthright self.

"What does it say?"

"Are you sure you…? Never mind. You wouldn't ask if you didn't…" Awkwardly, Liz read out, "Gemma Lawless. Died aged six years and two days. Twenty-two years ago. Blow to the head and drowned. Accidental death."

"Accidental death?"

"Yes, that's what it says. Is she your…?"

Interrupting, Brett replied desperately, "I don't know." He groaned and then said, "Thanks. That's all."

"Are you all right, Brett?"

"Fine. I've got to go now. Thanks again." He turned off the radio, closed his eyes, slumped in the seat and felt the tears trickling down his cheeks. He didn't know precisely why he was crying but he thought that he might be ashamed. He should not have forgotten such a momentous and tragic event in his family history. When he was five years old, something had happened to … a sister? Did he have a reason to feel guilt? Or just remorse? He didn't know. But he was sure that he had to go to see his parents. Major inquiry or not, he needed time.

"Time off!" Big John's boom could have been a question. More likely, it was an exclamation. "In case you hadn't noticed, we're in the middle of an escalating investigation."

"I'm asking for a day, two at the outside. I've got to go to my parents in Kent."

"Why?"

Brett paused and then explained, "A death in the family. A long time ago, I admit – when I was a youngster. I can't remember anything about it and my parents have never said anything." Brett nodded towards the glowing tent. "That brought it back to me. I need to know what went on. I think it was a sister – Gemma. Same age as Jayne."

Clare looked at him sympathetically, wanting to support him, but said nothing because she knew that she wouldn't have any influence over the boss.

John considered Brett's abrupt request. "You look awful," he answered at last. "I guess you're not much use to me if your mind's elsewhere. We'll call it compassionate leave. Go and sort yourself out. I want you back on the case within forty-eight hours. The locals'll tell you where you can go to hire a car."

"Thanks," Brett croaked.

"Take care," Clare said to him.

Big John turned away but then stopped and said over his shoulder, "Think on this, Brett. The message. *The world is taking notice of me now. Expect more news, Lawless.* He's killed a little girl just to tell you he's got everyone's attention. It makes your blood boil. And he's going to do it again. That should spur you back into action."

The cottage stood at the edge of an apple orchard,

familiar but somehow distant like a dream. On the outside of the weather-boarded bungalow, lapped white-washed wooden boards were mounted horizontally. Wisps of condensation and smoke rose lazily from the chimney. Brett had not seen his parents and his boyhood home in Kent for a year and a half. And before that … he couldn't put a date to it. He lingered outside, not daring to announce himself unexpectedly, as if he dreaded the visit. He did. His meetings with his mum and dad had always been strained. The truth was that all of his childhood with them – as much as he could recall – had been loveless and strained. He didn't relish what he now had to do.

For Brett, home had never been a refuge from a grim world. Even now, with the Messenger pursuing his evil career, home did not offer a safe retreat. When Brett summoned up the courage to push the bell, he felt awkward and unsettled. It was just like the emotion that he experienced when he was about to talk to the shattered family of a murder victim. This time, though, it was personal. This time, he was suffering greater turmoil. He was not sure that he would be able to cope with the coming conversation, but he could not sidestep it. He had to build a bridge over the chasm between himself and his parents – and he had to know about Gemma.

"Brett!" his father exclaimed, coming to the door. "What are you doing…?" He looked embarrassed. For a moment he seemed to be about to hold out his hand to his son but the token conciliatory gesture evaporated before it materialized. "Er... You'd better come in." Into the house, he called, "Kath! It's Brett."

Sitting uncomfortably, Brett surveyed the front room and his parents. In the fireplace burning logs crackled. For relaxation, his mum and dad probably gazed into the hypnotic fidgety flames just like Brett watched his meandering fish at home. The surface of every piece of his parents' furniture held antique china ornaments as delicate as Brett's mum. He'd never thought of his mum and dad as elderly before, but now they looked as ancient as the ornaments – much older than their years. They looked worn. His mother seemed to be permanently tired and fragile. Her hair was streaked with grey and she was thinner than Brett remembered. Brett's dad was just as big as ever – almost the same size as Brett – but firm muscle had been displaced by flabbiness. His looked like a body wasted.

Brett wrapped his hands round the hot mug of coffee that his dad had given him and said, "This is welcome after a long drive – a drink in front of a real fire."

"What brings you here?" his mum asked. "You wouldn't come all this way without good reason. It's not just a social visit," she surmised.

He peered into the brown steaming liquid and said, "No." He wasn't yet ready to ask his questions so he did not continue.

From a drawer, his father extracted coasters for

their mugs of coffee. To reach them, he had to move a large adjustable spanner that was in the same drawer.

Brett queried, "Why on earth have you got that in there?"

"There's been a good few burglaries recently. Your mum feels a bit more secure, knowing it's there."

"Well," Brett warned them, "be careful what you do with it or you'll be up on a charge of malicious wounding. You'll get a heavier sentence than the burglar."

"It's just a deterrent," his dad remarked. Nodding towards a newspaper in which Brett's investigation made front page headlines, he added, "You're involved in this terrible murder case. We've seen your name mentioned."

Brett nodded. "I'm not in charge any more. Too big. I'm second-in-command, if you like."

"A while ago you said on the phone you were taking on the bizarre cases," his mum recalled. "You had a knack for them, you thought."

"Yes. But this one's … troublesome."

"So we gathered," Brett's father put in.

There was an awkward silence. Brett wasn't sure if they wanted to move the conversation on or if they were waiting for him to explain the intricacies of the case. He decided not to linger on it. "Anyway," he said, "how are you both?"

His mother shrugged as his father murmured, "Fine."

"Not at work today?"

"I worked Saturday," his dad answered, "so I got today off."

"When do you retire?" Brett asked.

"In the summer. Early retirement."

There was another lapse in the exchange and Brett sipped his coffee. "Mmm. Good."

"Hadn't you better tell us what you're here for?" his mum prompted.

Brett exhaled and then drew in a deep breath. "I guess so," he agreed. "I, er, want you to tell me about Gemma."

He might as well have exploded a bomb in the front room. It would have had a similar devastating effect. Something had happened over twenty years ago and the memory of it still had the power to crush them. His mum was reduced to a quivering bundle of nerves and his father was stiff with apprehension and shock. Brett glanced from one to the other and murmured, "Sorry but I have to know what happened. Don't you think it's time we talked about it?"

His parents gazed at each other, then his dad looked at him and mumbled, "I think we knew this day would come. We couldn't face it before."

"But you will now?"

"We'd rather not," he replied in a hesitant voice, "but if we do, we'll tell you the truth, Brett. Are you sure *you* can face it?"

Brett grimaced but nodded. "I need to know."

Reluctantly, his father took the lead. His words

had to be forced from somewhere deep inside him where he'd buried his sorrow. "It was a Sunday, two days after your sister's sixth birthday. You were a year younger. You went out to play together, through the orchard and down by the river. Across from the golf course."

Brett noticed that his mum's eyes were wet with tears. He didn't know if she was weeping because of the painful memory of her daughter or because the tragedy was about to be revealed to her son.

"The two of you took one of Gemma's birthday presents – a small bike. After her birthday she wouldn't be separated from it. Truth be told, you were jealous, Brett. You would've got one of your own for your next birthday, but you were impatient." His father swallowed and continued, "Patience was never your strong point. We don't know exactly what happened – you never owned up. But, from the garbled version you gave at the time, we've got a pretty good idea. You probably fell out with your sister. Gemma wanted to go on her bike, you wanted to take it off her. Silly, wasn't it? There was an argument. I can just imagine Gemma stamping her foot and crying, 'It's mine!' and you using your greater strength – even at that age – to wrench the bike away from her."

Brett didn't really need the rest of the story but he sat in silence, crumpled, waiting to hear the inevitable end to his own selfishness. His mum buried her face in a handkerchief.

"There was a tussle of some sort. You admitted that you pushed her, that's all – we don't know exactly why or how. Probably pushed her off the bike. She landed awkwardly, cracking her head on a branch." His voice broke but he was intent upon reaching the end of the story – a story that he had concealed for twenty years, a story he might never mention again. "They found her blood on it later. She must have been knocked out, concussed. She rolled down the bank and into the river. Her body was found about a mile downstream."

Brett stared at the cold drink in his mug. He hardly dared to look up. He shook his head and sobbed, "I don't remember. I don't remember any of it. I saw the body of a young girl with a head wound yesterday and something clicked. I don't know how but somehow I knew about Gemma." He also re-membered becoming light-headed when Anna Stimpson mentioned the blow to Nicola Morrison's head, and when he'd joked with Clare that he had never resorted to murder. And the rivalry among his tropical fish had made him faint. All of these things had reached further into his mind than he'd realized. They had touched something suppressed in his sub-conscious and now it had been brought to the surface again. "So it wasn't an accident at all," Brett moaned. "I meant to…" He ground to a halt. He couldn't say aloud that he was a killer himself.

"We tried to forgive you, Brett. Lord knows we tried. We still do. But…" His mum whispered through her handkerchief, "She was a lovely happy girl. With us one moment and whisked away the next. We loved you, Brett, but we couldn't forgive."

"Or forget," her husband added.

"But *I* forgot!" Brett cried. "Why didn't you tell me? Why didn't you talk to me before?"

"We couldn't talk about it. It was too painful. Look at us even now," his dad replied emotively. "Re-living it is terrible. Bottling it up was our way of coping. Besides, you'd buried the memory. Not saying anything spared you from knowing. It was best for us *and* for you. We erased all memory of her from the house apart from… Anyway, we protected you from the…"

"Guilt," Brett uttered. He was witnessing another wrecked family, but this time *he* was to blame for the wrecking. He'd been well below the age of criminal responsibility, but he was responsible. He had killed through envy – a trivial reason to end a life. But he couldn't recall what was in his mind when he pushed his sister from her new bike. Did he want to harm her or did he just want her off the bike? Was he so jealous that he just didn't consider that she might be hurt? He hoped that he'd been more thoughtless than vicious, but he couldn't be sure. He wanted to remember, desperately. He would have derived a little comfort if he could recollect the scene and discover that his motives weren't entirely evil. He put down the wasted coffee and buried his head in his hands. When he looked up again, he asked, "Was I really bad? Would I have *wanted* to hurt her?"

His parents, distant and silent, still could not find it in themselves to give him the reassurance that he needed. They did not answer. Either they really didn't know or they feared the worst.

Brett's dad murmured, "I don't want to make things worse but there's something you should see." He looked towards his wife and she nodded her consent. He went to the bedroom and returned with a large envelope. "We protected ourselves – and you – by eliminating Gemma from our lives, but... Anyway, we kept just one thing: her birthday photograph." He withdrew it carefully, lovingly, from the envelope and held it out with a trembling hand. With more warmth in his voice than Brett had ever heard before, his dad said, "Now you know – for better or for worse – do you want to see your sister?"

Brett breathed deeply and reached out for the photograph.

Brett felt wretched as he drove home to Sheffield. No matter where his thoughts wandered, they kept returning to that dreadful riverside scene of his childhood and his sister's innocent face. To distract himself – not that he believed that he deserved a distraction – he tried to list in his mind the solid and certain evidence on the Messenger. It was pitifully little. He – or she – was still averaging one killing every eight days. Was the timing significant? He had Ecstasy on his coat sleeve. Brett was sure that the drug had nothing to do with Bill. Had the Messenger been in Mixers when Ecstasy had changed hands? He had short, dark, straight hair. He was well built, not particularly tall or short, and fit enough to out-run a retired but powerful rower. Was he really a robust woman in disguise? He bought a variety of newspapers and travelled widely. Were the times, dates and locations of his journeys important? He was manipulative, strong and attention-seeking.

Was he any worse than the grasping five-year-old Brett? "Yes," Brett said aloud. "I grew up. I grew out of it." Even so, he could not shake off the shame.

The squad had lots of other information, like the behavioural profile, but none of it would satisfy Brett's scientific rigour.

The M25 gave way to the equally tedious M1. Brett drove at the speed limit and watched numerous cars hurtle recklessly past him. He broke his journey just once, calling in at a service station for a drink and to reconnoitre the shop. Looking along the lengthy rows of papers and magazines, he spotted all of the publications that the Messenger had used so far, including *Our Dogs*. They were so easy to obtain that they told Brett nothing. But sometimes the absence of a clue was in itself revealing. Forensics had not detected even one partial fingerprint on any of the calling cards. That meant that the Messenger was extremely careful, avoiding the obvious snares. The fact that his activities had resulted in so few clues suggested a thoughtful killer who was aware of the phenomenal power of forensic science.

Brett turned on the radio for the news. He was surprised by a sombre John Macfarlane explaining the bare minimum about the latest murder and issuing a bland description of the Messenger to give the impression that the team was close on his heels.

John ended with a plea for vigilance, not hysteria. Clearly, the new murder had not yielded any major new leads that John wished to share with the public. The Messenger was so professional that it was likely there were no new leads at all. Brett would have taken some consolation from the murders if, after each one, he was a step closer to the killer.

It was late when he got back to Sheffield. He went directly to Clare's house but all of her lights were off. Instead, he drove to her regular pub in Totley. There she was, tucking into a seafood salad and watching the live folk group. Swaying slightly to the music, she looked happy and deeply attractive. Brett was embarrassed to impose on her but, when she glimpsed him, she did not appear to be put out. She smiled and left the group of people at her table. "How are you?" she said, genuinely concerned. "You look tired."

"Hungry. In need of an update on events."

"Yeah," she said, "but how are *you*? How was the visit?"

He shrugged.

"I'll buy you a drink and a decent meal," Clare offered, "then it's back to my place for a chat. Yes?"

"OK. Thanks."

After the lively pub, Clare's house seemed quiet and intimate. "I'll open a bottle of wine," she said. "You look like you need it."

Swirling the blood-red liquid in its glass, Brett said gently, "You told me you once watched someone attack your dad with a knife – when you were thirteen. Do you remember it vividly?"

"Every second, yes. As clear as anything. Like I'd got it on video. I think it's because I was so helpless and it was all so traumatic. I think the guilt kept it in my mind as well."

"Guilt?" Brett queried.

"We'd gone out to get my birthday present. That's what the mugger took. Dad was knifed for my present. I couldn't defend him, either – I just stood there. I guess it was shock, fright, and not having a clue what to do. I should've tried to help, but I would've probably got myself stabbed as well. I still felt guilty afterwards. That's why I've remembered it so clearly, I think."

Brett felt marginally better. If he had been guilty of wanting to hurt or kill his sister, perhaps he would have recollected it. But maybe there comes a point when the guilt weighs so heavily that the brain suppresses the incident altogether.

"I thought we were going to talk about you," Clare said, "not me."

Brett sighed and swallowed some more wine. As the night advanced, he tried to keep his feelings in check while he confessed to his partner that he was carrying an even greater burden than hers.

Clare reached across and touched his hand. "That's … awful. But you can't torture yourself over a twenty-year-old prank that turned bad. And neither should your folks!" she said indignantly.

"They've had it rough," Brett responded, defending them.

"So, having lost one child, they decided to make up for it by rejecting the other."

"They were trying to protect me as well," Brett pointed out.

"It still doesn't make sense."

"I'm not sure that good sense always prevails when something so horrible happens. Perhaps the second casualty of a killing is common sense." Brett drew in a deep breath and muttered, "But I really need to know what was in my mind at the point when I pushed her. I hope I didn't whack her with a branch or something. I can't rule it out."

"You can't rule it in either," Clare replied quickly. "I don't think you should—"

"Let's talk about something else, Clare. I've just about had my fill of soul-searching. What about Jayne – another case without much hard evidence?"

Clare poured more wine before she briefed him. "We're a bit further forward. In Macclesfield we got a sighting of a blue car but no details. Someone dragged her into it from a remote lane between her school and home. Her sisters were walking home with her but they weren't paying enough attention." Clare paused before adding, "At least *their* parents aren't blaming them. I'm sure *they'll* stick together." Clare glanced at Brett and continued, "Anyway, a few minutes later she was taken where you saw her and killed by a single blow to the head."

"She must've struggled and scratched him getting in or out of the car," Brett remarked. "Any skin or blood under her fingernails?"

"Gloves," Clare answered despondently. "Cold day."

"What did he take from her?"

"The gloves. At least it wasn't anything morbid this time."

"Any news on the source of the words in his message?"

"Made up from newspapers again. This time, it was *The Independent* and *Racing Post*."

"*Racing Post*, eh? Where was Terry Purcell?"

"We don't know. Not at home. Surveillance lost him so he's still on the hit list. But there *is* some good news: we didn't get a handle on Golby, Anna Stimpson or Ian Lowe either, but we *can* eliminate the chap in Gloucestershire. He may be a nasty character but he didn't move from home. He's out of the reckoning."

"Is that it?" Brett asked.

"The Messenger's a smart cookie," Clare answered, sipping some more wine.

Brett glanced at his watch and, surprised, said, "Have you noticed the time?"

It had flown past. It was one-thirty in the morning.

"And I…" Brett held up his glass of wine.

"Yes, you're well over the limit. Don't worry," she said, "you can stay here. The spare room's not too much of a mess."

"Are you sure?"

"Yeah. Just this once."

"Up early in the morning," Brett mentioned. "I've got to take the car back to a hire company near the city centre."

"All right," Clare responded with a grin. "I can take a hint. I'll follow you in my car so I can drive you into work afterwards."

"That's not all," Brett admitted. "I need to call in at home as well."

"Don't tell me," muttered Clare, "the fish need feeding."

"In one," Brett said.

In the morning, the phone rang and rang. Clare was taking a shower so Brett decided to answer it. "Hello," he said, reciting her telephone number.

The caller hesitated and then asked, "Is that you, Brett?"

Brett recognized Big John's voice. "Yes, I'm back. Just about to come in and report for duty."

"When you do, remind me to ask what you're doing at Clare's. Right now, don't bother to come in. I want you and Clare in Luton."

"Not another one!" Brett exclaimed.

"No, but a near thing. We've got wind of a failed assault in the airport grounds. The woman concerned didn't report it at first but, with all the publicity about the case, she's begun to wonder if she's had a close shave with the Messenger. I want you and Clare to go and check it out. Get on the M1 and Liz will radio in the details."

"What makes you think it's the Messenger?"

"It happened on the tenth. That should've been one of his days before he hit Macclesfield instead. On top of that, he accidentally dropped a calling card. At last, a bit of carelessness. I'm tracing reports on where our suspects were at the time. You go and gather what you can from the woman he attacked. And remember, Brett, we're keeping a lid on the calling cards. We've kept his trademarks from the media. That's why she didn't realize who he was straightaway – she didn't know about the calling cards. So, find out his message but don't let on to the woman. We can't afford a leak. She might be thinking of selling her story to the press – the one that got away."

Kirsty O'Shea was about twenty with a round, homely face and long red hair. She was much shorter than Clare but, like Brett's partner, she was one of life's fighters.

"I'd just flown in from Edinburgh," she explained. "Business trip. The plane was half an hour late, delayed by fog. It was a filthy evening, dark, drizzly and foggy. Turbulent journey. We were supposed to get in at eight-thirty but it turned out to be nine. Anyway, I went to get my car, parked at the back end of that huge car park. Honestly, you could have all sorts going on in there and no one would see a thing.

I bent down to unlock the car and I got the feeling I was being watched. I turned round and he was right there. He went to grab me, but I had this heavy briefcase and I took a swipe at him. I caught him beautifully – winded him. I took another swing at him but he dodged it by diving to the ground. Amazing reflexes! Anyone normal wouldn't have got out of the way like that."

"Can you describe how he landed?" Clare asked, interrupting her flow.

Kirsty tapped her right shoulder. "He seemed to go down shoulder first, head tucked in. He rolled over and then got to his feet, like, all in one movement. Then he ran off."

Clare glanced at Brett and murmured, "Sounds to me like someone with a bit of judo training."

"Did he make for a car?" Brett enquired.

"Not as far as I could see," answered Kirsty, "but visibility was awful. He disappeared in seconds."

"We'll need to get videos from airport security cameras," Brett noted.

"What did he look like?" asked Clare. "Did you get a good look at his face?"

"You've got to be joking!" Kirsty exclaimed. "I was more into self-preservation than taking notes. It was dark and he had a hood on, and he had a scarf across much of his face. Threatening maybe but, in that weather, not out of place. I'll tell you one thing, though: when he dived out of the way, his scarf came away a bit. I didn't see much of the lower part of his face," she reported, sliding a hand across her mouth and chin, "but I did catch sight of a moustache."

Brett and Clare glanced at each other. "Can you be sure of that?" Brett asked. "It wasn't just a trick of the light or a shadow?"

"No, I'm pretty sure."

A moustache changed everything. It put a whole new slant on the investigation. None of their remaining suspects sported one.

"How tall was he?"

"Taller than me – by quite a bit. But I'm only small. He wasn't as tall as either of you."

"Age? Could you tell?"

"Not a hope."

They got a poor description of his clothes and physique from Kirsty and then Brett asked, "Did he say anything?"

"No," she replied. "Not a word."

"Not even a grunt when you hit him?" Clare enquired.

"Strangely not."

Clare looked puzzled but kept her thoughts to herself.

Eager to hear about the calling card as well, Brett continued, "We heard you spotted something on the ground where he dived."

"Oh, yes. I picked it up. I guess it could've been there all along but I thought it might have come out of his pocket when he rolled over. A small piece of card." She traced the usual size in the air. "Strange.

I read it by the internal light in the car. It was made up of headlines – you know. From a newspaper, I suppose."

"What did you do with it?"

"I brought it home but then threw it out."

"Have your bins been emptied since?"

"Yes. It'll have gone. Was it important?"

Brett shrugged. "Possibly. What did it say?"

"Something like, 'Maybe I should be called Lawless instead.' Hey," Kirsty said suddenly, "You said your name was Lawless. Surely it means something to you."

Brett grimaced. The Messenger was getting more personal. Of all the jokes on Brett's name, this was the sickest. "Not a great deal, I'm afraid."

"Oh. Pity. Well? What do you think? *Was* I attacked by this madman in the papers?"

Brett hated lying but he had to protect the investigation. He shook his head. "We'll be looking into it but it doesn't sound like our man. For one thing, he doesn't have a moustache. I think you had a lucky escape from a mugger. More interested in briefcases and purses than people's lives."

Their car full of videotapes with murky shots of a fog-bound Luton airport, they made their way back to Sheffield on the rain-swept motorway.

Brett put a different coloured drawing pin on the map at Luton. "Green for no kill," he announced, "but I think he meant to take another victim there. If the locations are important to him, he's just given us a free clue."

"And he might go back sometime to finish the job," Greg suggested.

John said, "I've got the locals to keep an eye on Kirsty O'Shea in case he's after particular victims – in case he goes back for another bite of the same cherry. But I doubt it. He's picking them randomly, I'm sure. That's what his profile says. Random – whoever's convenient."

"Then you'll have to barricade the town," Liz chipped in. "No bad thing to barricade Luton."

Brett wrote down the words from the missing calling card, then he pinned the piece of paper to the wall with the others. "We got another message free of charge as well."

"It's like the Macclesfield one – another aimed at you, Brett," John declared. "Another Lawless joke. Not very helpful."

Liz interjected, "You can kiss another suspect goodbye. I got Purcell's minders in Cambridge to sneak a look at the milometer in his car. He just hasn't done enough mileage for trips to Luton *and* Macclesfield. Unless, unknown to our crew, he's used another car or the train or something, he's in the clear."

"Ian Lowe hasn't been seen at all," John added. "I've got every force on alert, looking out for him. Lance Golby's on the road too much to follow – we can only watch him come and go. There's never been a murder – or attempted murder – when he's stayed at home. Bad luck for him or... Anyway, he went to north London by car on the tenth. It all checks out. The company he visited confirmed that he was there. But he left in time to be in Luton at about nine. We've got his car on M1 cameras. We've tracked it all the way back, even in the fog down south that night. There's a missing half hour in the Luton area. Golby says he called in at Toddington service station between junctions 11 and 12. It fits, but so would calling in at Luton airport. And, Brett, you said he was going to Luton airport before – to do something to their computer. Perhaps that was when he scouted out the place. And on the twelfth – Macclesfield day – he took a day off. Went walking in the Peaks, he said. No alibi."

Greg joined in. "Anna Stimpson was away as well. Used the train. On the tenth she bought a return ticket for London and she returned on the thirteenth. She's telling a tale about touring round theatres and clients. It seems to check out but there's gaps without explanations. She's still up there."

"Golby, Lowe and Stimpson – I've had their rubbish intercepted," Big John informed Brett. "Some poor coppers won't thank me for it. They've been through the trash but there's no sign of cut-up papers or anything else incriminating." He slumped into a chair and muttered, "It's not enough, Brett. We might knock those last three off the list – then who do we follow? We'd be lost. We need something positive. I've got people visiting newsagents in routine enquiries. I'm running checks on travellers, sales-people, road haulage companies – anyone who travels a lot. No joy. I need something from you, Brett. I need inspired ideas."

"You need another fact as well," Brett commented. "They're *all* off the list already," he groaned. "Kirsty O'Shea tells us he's got a moustache."

"A moustache!"

"Looks like he tried to cover it up but his scarf was dislodged and she spotted it."

John cursed. "There's not much point carrying on with the surveillance," he grumbled. "Have we had any suspects with a moustache?"

"Only one witness who put himself forward. Seems like an eternity ago. Andrew Laughton, insurance salesman. Nothing at all to incriminate him, apart from a moustache of questionable taste."

"All right," John said. "Now I *do* need some serious inspiration from you, Brett," he repeated. "But right now, go and see Keith Johnstone. He wants you and Clare in his office. Lack of progress and the whiff of scandal always brings him to life."

16

The desk-bound Chief Superintendent leaned forward. "Time's running out, Brett," he declared. "It's running out for his next victims and," he added bluntly, "for your probationary period. I need progress. I need an arrest."

Brett was taken aback by the Chief's comment. He took a moment to inhale then replied calmly, "We're doing all we can against an apparently random killer. Without logic, he's difficult to catch."

"There's always a logic, even if it's warped. It's just that you haven't pinned it down yet. More work, less holiday. Clare, you're supposed to be good at getting inside people, at seeing motives, and no doubt you're thinking this is the sort of high-profile case that can help promotion. You'd be right. Let's see both of you tidying it up. Soon." He rested his arms on his desk. "I also want to take this opportunity to review your partnership. John tells me that you're a good team. He sticks by you. What do you think?"

Clare and Brett glanced at each other, puzzled. "Fine, sir," Clare put in. "It's going well."

Keith gazed at Brett and said, "You can be frank with me."

"I, er, think we enjoy working together," Brett replied.

"Working together," Keith repeated slowly. "Good. We like to preserve a good working partnership. But when you go into a dangerous situation – as you inevitably will sometimes – I want you acting correctly, thinking about your roles as police officers and your responsibility for the safety of the public. You shouldn't be thinking about each other. At least, not outside the normal care and concern for a colleague. A professional relationship, yes, but nothing else. Do you follow me?"

Clare and Brett were both frowning. "Yes, sir," they said.

"I won't hesitate to break up the party if you two embark on an unprofessional relationship."

"But—"

Interrupting Brett, the Chief said, "I don't want to hear any denials or anything else. I just want you to absorb what I've said and act accordingly. That's it."

They understood that they were dismissed so they turned and left his office. In the corridor, Brett cursed, annoyed at the false accusation of forming an improper relationship. Clare could see the funny side of it. Teasing him, she said, "I hope you're not annoyed because you're ashamed to be caught having an affair with me – even though you're not. That would be grossly insulting."

"No," Brett exclaimed. "Of course not. I'd be…"

"What?"

"Never mind."

Still baiting him, Clare hung an arm on his shoulder and said, "Next time, *I'll* answer the phone – or let the answering machine take care of it." Then she smiled. "Forget it. There was a more important warning in there. About the case."

Brett nodded. "I could hardly miss it: more work, more inspiration, more arrests."

Clare whispered, "It's not really about my career or yours. It's his. I heard he's up for chief constable in some other force. He doesn't want an unsolved and awkward case to make him look ineffective. Solving it would be a feather in *his* cap."

"What about John's, or yours – or mine?"

"You've got to be joking! John might come out of it well, but we're just the workers."

On the morning of Sunday 18th February, Brett punished himself with a tough run around the park. As he pounded along the path beside the lake, the disturbed ducks scattered in disarray, most of them plopping into the water. It might be Sunday, but for

Brett it was going to be an ordinary working day. Not really ordinary. Any day on which the Messenger was due to kill could never be described as ordinary. But who? And where?

Brett had showered and was halfway through breakfast when his pager called him to the next murder. An early-morning jogger just like himself, killed with unprecedented, sickening force in Grantham.

Brett threw on his coat and headed for the door. Before he left, he glanced back into the kitchen. The Magic Eye picture on his fridge door caught his eye and stopped him in his tracks. Suddenly, unexpectedly, he saw it. The illusion was no longer a frustrating web of images. A clown was smiling insanely at him from a distance. No doubt, it was supposed to be a funny face but Brett saw in it an expression that he associated with the Messenger – a cruel smile. He pointed his finger at the deceptive joker and muttered, "At last! I can see you!" Then he dashed out of the house, leaving a half-drunk mug of coffee.

When the pathologist showed them the wound, Brett winced. The jogger was no weakling but his ribcage had been crushed with one well-directed and angry kick.

"Amazing power," the pathologist said. "I've never seen anything like it. Caved in. But it was definitely a kick. Right angle and I can almost take an imprint of a shoe from the bruise."

Brett said, "This is your territory, Clare." He was referring to her skills at karate. "Have *you* ever seen anything like this?"

"No," she answered, utterly appalled. "It's incredible. It shouldn't happen. It must've been done by an expert but we're trained *not* to do this. Anyone advanced enough to do it must have amazing strength, coordination and self-control. So, where did the self-control go? In any fight, there's no need to let loose a blow like this if you're good enough to do it. See what I mean? That's the irony. The more you learn, the less you have to use it. At his level, he could incapacitate anyone without permanent harm." Choked, she said, "I guess we have a furious, out-of-control expert."

John put in, "We're seeing a new side to him – learning all the time. But I suppose it's consistent with the single blows he dealt out to Jayne in Macclesfield and Nicola Morrison. He's clinical."

At last Brett understood how the Messenger had outpaced Terry Purcell in Cambridge. He was exceptionally fit.

They were standing on the perimeter of a golf course to the north of Grantham. Behind them was a quiet minor road, just off the A52 that led to Staffordshire in one direction and the Lincolnshire coast in the other. Brett asked his partner, "Which discipline would teach you how to inflict this sort of damage?"

"Oh, in theory, any one of several martial arts. But,

as I said, a killing blow shouldn't ever happen. I've never seen it done and I wish I hadn't now. It's totally against the philosophy. It's a capability like a nuclear weapon: extreme strength that's meant to keep the peace by not being used."

"I leave it to you, Clare, to tour the karate clubs and run checks on dodgy members," John told her.

"Of course," Clare replied, still ashen-faced with the shock of discovering the use – the abuse – of terminal force. She was always dismayed by murder but this one really rankled. The killer had broken all the rules of her favourite recreation.

"And if you come across him," John added, "keep your distance."

"I'll tell you something," Brett said, "this picture of him as an expert fighter doesn't square with the handbagging he got at Luton."

"You're right," Clare said, suddenly animated. "He wouldn't have allowed himself to be winded – or hit in the first place!"

"What are you two saying?" John asked. "We've got a different man? Impossible. We can't have a copycat at Luton because no one knows about the calling cards – except the Messenger – so it must've been him."

"There *is* another explanation," Brett replied. "Maybe he was playing games at Luton. He never meant to harm Kirsty. He *allowed* her to beat him off."

"That's why he didn't grunt when Kirsty O'Shea

thought she'd winded him," Clare said. "Because she hadn't. He was acting. But why?"

Brett thought about it for a moment and then answered, "To throw us into confusion. He *wanted* us to know about the moustache."

John was nodding. "Anna Stimpson," he muttered. "You think it's her and she's manipulating us. We're supposed to be tricked into thinking the Messenger's a man with a moustache. It was a false, theatrical one."

"It's a bit elaborate, but it's possible," Brett agreed. "But not just Anna Stimpson. Anyone can stick on a false moustache and let a witness get a peep at it. Maybe it means we're getting close and he – or she – decided to try and fool us. Really it's a woman or a clean-shaven man."

"It fits his profile," John remarked. "It would amuse him to send us down a blind alley."

"It's already worked," Clare pointed out. "We withdrew surveillance from the top three on the basis of the moustache. We don't know where they are now or where they were when the Messenger put his foot into this man's ribs."

One of the forensic team handed the latest calling card to John. It was sealed in a transparent evidence bag and this time the message was very brief. *End of the line*.

"End of the line…" Brett muttered thoughtfully to himself.

"Mean anything to you?" asked John.

Brett shrugged. "If only. But at least this one's worth thinking about. Not just a declaration about publicity."

"It sounds like the end again. Similar to *I am complete*," John mused. "But that wasn't the end, and I dare say this won't be either."

"Any witnesses this time?" Clare enquired.

"No," John answered. "Too early in the morning."

"Who found him?"

"No one. Or rather, one of the local uniforms. The victim's wife called when he didn't return from his jog, apparently." John wiped his moist brow and proclaimed, "I always knew jogging's no good for the health." John would have struggled to walk at a fast pace, never mind break into a run. "Anyway," he said, "she was on edge because of the newspaper reports. Phoned the police. A quick search by beat officers located him. As with the others, he wasn't exactly hidden."

Brett asked the forensic scientist if he'd found anything that might prove helpful but the white-suited man shook his head. "A bit early to be sure but it looks clean."

The pathologist, appearing to be praying over the victim, looked up and said, "You know, seriously, I might be able to do something for you. It's not much but I might just get you his shoe size from this wound."

"Good. And, er, is anything missing?" Brett asked, dreading the answer.

"Oh, yes," the pathologist replied with a pained expression. "I take comfort from the fact that the dead don't need both little fingers."

The team studying the videos from Luton airport assembled a sequences of images of people who fitted Kirsty's description of her attacker. When Greg played her the tape, she identified her assailant in a sequence lasting just a few seconds. "That's him! I think so, anyway." He had been captured on video as he walked through the car-park exit at 9:21pm, but it wasn't a clear view. He was wrapped up like a mummy and the fog blurred the image. Greg handed over the tape to the video unit where the picture would be enhanced, the figure defined as fully as possible and his size calculated.

Clare's instructor put down the photograph without speaking. He examined the unwelcome image, glanced at his long-standing pupil and then looked back at the photograph with distaste. "It's a travesty," he said, pushing away the horrifying image of death.

"Exactly," Clare murmured. "Even by police-force standards, we're seeing things no one should have to see. But who's capable of such a thing?"

"Well, I know a few who *could*. I don't know any who *would*. It's against everything we teach."

"Quite," Clare responded. "It means we're looking for a rogue. Any ideas? You must have come across some funny folk wanting to take up martial arts."

"Yes. And I've rejected them all. All the ones with dodgy motives for learning."

"Are there any dodgy clubs around who'd not ask questions and take on anyone?"

"There used to be, perhaps, but they've been weeded out."

"Couldn't he have learned at one of those some time ago?" Brett asked.

"Possibly," the trainer answered. "But to deliver a blow like this," he said, nodding towards the photograph but not wanting to look at it again, "he'd have to have regular practice. Difficult without a club to go to."

"So he's not from round here," Brett deduced, "or he's fooled everyone into thinking he's perfectly normal when he isn't." Brett paused before adding, "And when I say *he*, I mean he or she."

"Mostly men," the instructor said. "Only a few women – like Clare here."

"Anyone called Anna Stimpson? Muscular woman, middle-aged."

The trainer shook his head.

"Ian Lowe? Lance Golby?" Brett enquired.

"No. They don't mean anything to me," he said. "There's a problem here because everyone I know who could do this is beyond suspicion. They just wouldn't. They're … too good. There's a couple in the county team. There's at least one police officer, one lawyer and me. It's not worth giving you a list – even if I was prepared to do so – because they're calm, level-headed, caring people. I think you'd better look at the hard schools outside this club and probably beyond Sheffield."

"Hard schools?" Brett queried.

Clare answered him. "Those emphasizing power and strength. Soft schools go for speed and precision."

"Looks like our man's got all four," Brett ventured.

Brett and Clare traipsed round the clubs and heard similar sentiments expressed by all of them. None had Ian Lowe, Lance Golby or Anna Stimpson as members. When they had finished in Sheffield, they drove to Worksop. There were only a few clubs and the third bore fruit. The International Tae Kwon Do Martial Arts Centre was much less refined than its name suggested. It occupied a basement in a backstreet. The oriental owner spoke in stilted English with a marked Korean accent.

"Lowe, you say. I know this man. His father brought him." Tapping the left side of his chest, he said, "His heart is not in it. A father wants a son to be strong but a son – he might not wish the same. Ian Lowe, I can give him feet of steel, but that not what he needs. I cannot give him confidence. He can never be complete. What use is physical strength without inner strength?"

"When did he first come to you?"

"Two years ago."

Brett asked, "Did he learn Tae Kwon Do to any extent?"

The master of the club hesitated. "How to explain?" he murmured, almost to himself. "He learn a few moves but without heart and a balanced, untroubled mind…" He shook his head dismally. "No good."

Clare nodded. "I still have to ask you," she said putting her right hand on her ribcage, "could he break a bone?"

The small Korean gazed for a moment into Clare's face. "I would like to teach you," he declared with a smile. "You *know*. You have the spirit."

Clare returned his smile graciously. "Thank you. But the bone?"

"He does not look strong. Ian Lowe, he will never be strong. Not truly strong. But his feet can speak."

"Speak?" Brett muttered with a frown.

"If he wish to converse with an enemy, he can use his feet. But as for bone, it is more resolute than Ian's mind."

"Have you seen him in the last week or so?" Clare checked.

"No. I see him last a month ago."

"So he *has* kept practising, even after his father died."

"He practise more since his father die. He wants not to be bullied again." He shrugged, suggesting that Ian could not escape his problems through Tae Kwon Do. "He still not strong. Strength is here," he said, pointing to his head. Lifting a bare foot he added, "Not here."

Brett took away the impression that Ian Lowe was not as helpless as he looked and perhaps not as feeble as the martial arts trainer had indicated. Brett did not believe that he'd need formidable confidence and peace of mind to strike a formidable blow. Clare was more understanding. She knew the character and self-belief that went into such an act. If the attacker did not believe absolutely that he could aim at a point behind the ribs and hit hard enough to reach it – to slice through bone as if it were paper – then he would not succeed. That sort of strength *was* in the mind, and she did not believe that Ian Lowe possessed it.

Back at headquarters, facts were arriving in the incident room. The words in the Grantham message had been culled from the magazine *New Scientist*. The shoe of the killer was almost certainly size nine. The video technician had measured the height of the man leaving Luton airport car park. She had used the passing Ford Mondeo in the same shot to scale the pictures. Taking camera angle into account, her best estimate was five feet ten. Enhancement and enlargement of his face had revealed little. The image was more woolly than the scarf that covered most of his face. His hood and the fog obscured the rest.

"How tall is Ian Lowe?" John enquired.

"Five feet ten?" Brett suggested, looking questioningly at Clare.

"Yeah," she agreed. "That's what I'd say. Like Anna Stimpson."

"And Lance Golby," Brett added.

"Even so," John uttered, "the evidence is building against Ian Lowe. Since he's disappeared off the face of the earth, he can't invite us into his house, but I think we need to take a look inside. We've got good grounds for a warrant. I'll see to it. Let's see if we can find a collection of sick trophies."

"I don't think you missed your career," Big John observed as he watched Greg fiddle about inside the lock on Ian Lowe's door. "If you'd taken up burglary, you'd have been arrested before you got inside your first house."

"If I'd taken up burglary, I would've been in by now. Brick through the back window."

"Not very elegant," John retorted. "Do you want me to call in the big blokes with a ram?"

"No … just a minute. Something's…" Inside the lock there was a satisfying click and Greg stood upright with a smile on his face. "Something's given. After you, Boss," he said flamboyantly.

Ian Lowe's country house admitted the squad that John had assembled. A musty smell emanated from the interior as if they had just opened a sealed tomb.

John stepped inside and grimaced. "Not very efficient with duster and vacuum cleaner, our Mr Lowe," he remarked.

The place was filthy. Mould was growing around the window frames, cobwebs matted the lampshades, and every surface was thick with dust. "I wonder if he's cleaned it since his father died," Brett muttered.

It looked and smelled like a house that had been empty for months but in the large lounge, there were last week's newspapers – and ones from weeks before. "Look at this," Clare breathed. She was pointing to whole piles of papers and magazines that were stacked untidily by the sofa.

"Interesting," John murmured.

Big John asked the photographer to record the undisturbed room before telling a couple of his officers to flick through every newspaper and magazine, listing all of the publications and searching for cut-out headlines.

Clare's eye was drawn to a bookshelf. There was a book of poetry, lying on its side, with a piece of paper marking a particular page. She opened it up and sighed. "Jacques Prévert," she announced. "I know his work. Street poet of his day. Went straight for the guts. Listen. This one starts, 'There are great puddles of blood on the world.' Someone's underlined these bits. 'It doesn't give a damn, the earth, it turns, it doesn't stop turning, and the blood doesn't stop running… Where's it going, all this spilled blood? Murder's blood… war's blood… misery's

191

blood [...] the blood of children calmly tortured by their papa and their mama.' Powerful but not very uplifting."

"Mmm," John muttered. He said nothing but he was becoming increasingly bothered by Ian Lowe's state of mind.

Brett suggested, "Ian probably singled it out because of the beatings dished out by his father. It doesn't necessarily make Ian himself a spiller of blood."

"True," Clare agreed. "You don't *have* to be a raving psychopath to like Prévert. I read him sometimes. But even so…"

The rest of the team swarmed over the large but dingy property like termites. In a sideboard there was a large hoard of old coins and postcards. Seeing it, Clare said to Brett, "I told you he'd be a collector of something." The kitchen was a health hazard. In one cupboard, the vegetables were grey and mouldy. The crockery and cutlery remained unwashed, encrusted with unrecognizable scraps. Much of the remaining food was past its best-before date. There was an infestation of woodlice in the dining area, as well as some other insects that the cameraman did not recognize but photographed anyway. The main bedroom, once occupied by Charles Lowe, had been wrecked. Every piece of furniture had been smashed, ornaments mangled and clothes cut mercilessly. Charles' army uniform had been shredded with particular venom. Clare groaned when she noticed the slashed painting. She recognized it as the weird and wonderful work of one of her favourite surrealists, René Magritte, and its destruction pained her. It seemed that Ian had taken his revenge on his father after he died. Ian's own bedroom was untidy but not damaged. The bedclothes were disarrayed and dirty but they had not acquired much dust. The bed had been used recently. The shoes scattered in the wardrobe were size nine. Two of the team rummaged in the loft, their torches probing every corner, but it appeared not to have been disturbed for years.

After three hours of meticulous searching, John admitted that they were not going to find a collection of murderous souvenirs in the house or garage. And the newspapers had not been hacked by scissors. There were no copies of *Our Dogs*, *Angling Times* or *Racing Post* in Ian's pile but all of the other newspapers and magazines that the Messenger had used were there. John didn't expect to find gashes in them. After all, the Messenger was clever. He wouldn't leave such damning evidence lying in an abandoned house. Yet there was no doubt at all that it was the home of a seriously disturbed individual. John vowed to step up the search for Ian Lowe.

The radio burst into crackling, frantic life. It was Liz's voice. "We've just had another murder in Worksop," she reported urgently. "In the centre. A knifing. This time we've got a fix on the culprit. He's driving a blue Astra and he's headed your way. The A57 towards Sheffield. Registration Neil 515 Victor

Victor Alpha. Two Notts traffic-control cars are right behind him. If you block the road where you are, right now, you've got him. You'll have to shift, though."

John's eyes told Brett to get moving.

Brett and Clare sprinted out of the house, shouting for three other drivers to follow them. "Block the A57! My car's unmarked so put yours either side of me so it's clear there's a police roadblock," Brett shouted. "Move!"

Clare leapt into the driver's seat. She was already pulling away when Brett dived in through the passenger's side. "Go!"

Three panda cars and Clare's unmarked vehicle screeched down Ian Lowe's driveway. With horns blaring, the small convoy turned left at speed into North Anston lane. It was about a mile to the main road. Clare put her foot down and threw the car at each corner. Brett was murmuring, "Come on, come on!" as if he could make the car go faster. The nearside tyres ran on to the soft verge and kicked mud noisily at the wheel arches. Brett ignored it. Clare jerked the steering wheel and the car lurched back on to the tarmac. Within ninety seconds, she brought the car to the edge of the A57. As far as they knew, the blue Astra had not gone past. Without hesitation, Clare drove the car across the carriageway. A panda car came alongside, its light flashing, and the other two pandas completed the roadblock, making an angle between the kerbs and the cars parked across the white line.

Into the radio, Brett shouted, "In position. Have we trapped him?"

John replied, "We've got a bird above him. Look out for it, then you'll know."

They got out and looked to the sky while the uniformed officers were flagging down cars. "There," Brett uttered, pointing. "The helicopter. We've got him!"

The killer was heading straight into a traffic jam.

Brett could hear the sirens of the traffic-control cars, shepherding the killer into a dead-end. "Come on," Brett said to Clare. "Let's go get him."

They began to jog back down the line of cars that had formed. Clare dashed along the kerb and Brett ran along the white line. At least two drivers leaned out of their windows and shouted, "What's going on, mate?" Brett ignored them. He would have been happier if he had been leading a team of ten, but there was no time to organize it. Two would have to do. At least he wasn't on his own, and there was no one better than Clare in situations like this.

The helicopter almost seemed to be hovering above them. No doubt it was videoing the action. At the end of the stationary cars, Brett and Clare stopped and waited. There was a bend in the road in front of them. There would not be much warning when the Astra came round it. The car was bound to be travelling fast. The sirens of the police vehicles were screaming now. Any moment and...

Brett opened the door of the last car. Showing his

identification, he barked, "Out!" He didn't have time for niceties. He grabbed the woman's arm and yanked her out into the road. He was concerned in case the murderer crashed into the back of her car and shunted it forward. He didn't want any more casualties than necessary.

"What…?" the driver spluttered, stunned and confused.

"Just take cover. Over there! Away from the road." He propelled her towards the kerb.

In shock, she did what she was told.

Over her car, Brett and Clare scrutinized each other's faces without speaking. They were both nervous, excited and fearful. But they didn't have time to dwell on their own feelings. They had a job to do. And the Astra hurtled round the bend, coming straight at them like a ferocious charging animal. N515 VVA. It was obvious that it wasn't going to stop in time. Brett and Clare took cover and the woman driver screamed.

At the last moment, the Astra driver decided to try to drive down the empty right-hand side of the road. He didn't quite make it. His car swerved and the back end clipped the woman's stationary car. There was a stomach-churning thud as metal buckled and twisted. The man in the driving seat was flung first one way and then the other as his car was kicked into a spin. It bounced and rotated through three hundred and sixty degrees, ending up facing forward in the wrong lane. Brett and Clare sprinted towards the car but it took off again. The helicopter still hovered overhead like a bird of prey. The traffic-control cars, arriving on the scene in a blaze of flashing lights, stopped in the right-hand lane, plugging the only hole. The culprit was completely blocked in. He accelerated, not realizing that the road was blocked round the next bend.

Brett and Clare ran after the Astra, ready to arrest him as soon as he saw that he was hopelessly caged.

"Oh, no!" Brett groaned as he ran. The car was still gaining speed. The driver had obviously decided to batter his way through the cordon. Up ahead, the three officers scattered for cover.

The Astra sank into one of the panda cars with a horrifying crunch. It was shunted several metres down the road but it still barred the way. It looked as if the driver had tried to compress two cars into one twisted mess.

Panting, Brett arrived at what had been the Astra's door. Inside, the man lay still, his head at a ludicrous angle and some blood on his face. Brett had never seen him before but he was wearing a moustache. Brett pulled on the handle but the deformed door would not budge.

Clare yanked on the other side but it was just as badly warped and obstinate. She pointed to the flames that had begun to stroke the sills of the gnarled vehicle. "Brett! Get clear! It's going to blow."

"Just a second." He tried the rear door. It was distorted in its frame but it did open. Brett could feel the warmth inside. Underneath, the fire was heating it like a frying pan. Quickly, he adjusted the driver's seat into a nearly horizontal position and, summoning all of his strength, tugged the unconscious man by his shoulders. Unceremoniously, Brett dragged him out of the rear door. His feet hit the surface of the road heavily and his trousers caught fire.

Brett thought that Clare had retreated to a safe distance but she was there, stripping off her coat and throwing it over the man's legs to smother the flames. Then she bent down, grabbed him by the feet and lifted. With their cumbersome load, Brett and Clare hurried away as best they could. As soon as they had staggered a few metres from the car, it exploded. They were thrown forward, landing with pained grunts on the grass verge.

The helicopter had flown some distance away to avoid being caught in the updraft. Both the panda car and the Astra were consumed in the blaze.

"That was midway between daft and heroic," Clare said to Brett in admiration. "You could've been fried in an attempt to rescue a dead man."

"Call an ambulance!" Brett shouted to the police officers before he examined the man's inert body. In the wrecked car, he'd thought that he had seen a flicker of life in the driver's pallid face. Feeling his neck carefully, Brett said, "This dead man's got a pulse. Just."

"OK," Clare whispered. "You could've been fried in an attempt to rescue a mass murderer. I know a few people who'd have paid you not to try so hard."

"He's not guilty yet. And even if he is the Messenger…"

"Yeah, yeah," Clare interrupted. "I know. You play it by the book. But Leanne's parents and Jayne's family might see it differently. Anyway, do you know who he is? Have you seen him before?" she enquired, peering at the man, still out cold.

Brett shook his head. "No idea."

"How are you?" she asked him. "OK? You've got a good bruise." She touched her own cheek.

Brett's fingertips explored the bump on his face and then he murmured, "I'm all right." Even so, he rubbed his left elbow and aching ribs, and stretched each of his limbs to make sure he'd not broken anything.

Clare had landed perfectly – like a cat. "At least it's all over," she said, with a sigh of relief. "Just like that."

Brett gazed up at the sky and murmured, "Yeah. All of a sudden, the world's a bit brighter."

It seemed almost too easy. Almost an anticlimax.

Clare glanced upwards as well and said, "Brett? I never asked you. Do *you* think there's anyone up there, keeping a fatherly eye on us?"

"I'm certain. The helicopter pilot," he replied, deliberately misunderstanding her question.

Clare laughed. It was the carefree and abandoned reaction of someone who had just captured a serial killer. "You know what I mean," she said, still chuckling.

"It's hard when people like him," Brett replied, nodding towards the pale, motionless man beside them, "commit such awful crimes. When kids..." Brett stopped. He was thinking of Gemma as well as Jayne and Leanne.

More sober, Clare muttered, "Yeah. Somehow, I don't think this one's bound for heaven when he goes."

Brett and Clare were still having check-ups in hospital when Brett's mobile phone demanded attention. "I know I gave you both the rest of the day to recover," John said, "but, when you're finished there, I want you down here. Worksop. I'm looking at the victim. I want you and Clare to look at him as well."

"Why? What's the problem?"

"Something tells me there's another twist to this one yet." His tone suggested annoyance.

"OK," Brett replied. "We'll be with you as soon as we can."

"On our deathbeds," Clare muttered wryly.

The killer had been disturbed in a backstreet of Worksop by an off-duty Nottinghamshire police officer with a mobile phone. As a result, there was no calling card and no memento had been taken. The killer did not have the time – he had just fled. At least, that was one explanation for the absence of the Messenger's MO, but there was another.

Brett and Clare took one look at the victim's face and groaned.

"Well?" Big John prompted.

"This isn't the Messenger's work," Brett proclaimed with a miserable sigh.

"It's the drug squad's informant," Clare explained. "Stuart Dundee."

"Otherwise known as Croc," Brett added.

"I didn't think it smelled right," John said. "The

201

fools left him out in the big cruel world for too long. Dealers deal pretty swiftly with double-crossers. If your bloke with the moustache survives – thanks to Brett – you can question him if you like, but he isn't our Messenger, with or without a moustache. He's just been hired by the pushers to remove a traitor. That's all. Full stop." As the pathologist zipped up the body bag, John muttered, "There goes the case against the pushers. What a mess!" he grumbled. "Still, now it's not the Messenger it's not our problem. Over to Nottinghamshire. Even so, I think I'll have a serious word with Chief Inspector Smith."

Brett could guess what the word would be.

"Come on," John said. "I've had enough of squabbles between drug barons. We've got a *real* job to do."

"Here he is," John said, holding up an enlarged photograph for the team to see. "Not a pretty sight. It's the best likeness of him we found in his house. There's pocket-sized copies for all of you and Liz has sent it electronically to every force in the land. I want this man. And I want every beat officer in the country to have this picture – and the details of his car – in mind all the time. Ian Lowe. Twenty-three years old, a bad stammer and an even worse complexion. Five feet ten. Despite appearances, he might be deadly with his feet, so no one should tackle him alone. But finding him's our top priority. He could be anywhere but he's our number-one suspect."

Greg Lenton called, "Are you going back to the media? Are you getting the public in on the act of finding him?"

"No," Big John replied. "Imagine the media's reaction! Like a pack of hounds. They'll dig up anything and everything on him. Because we want to question him, every headline'll shout he's guilty, he did it. If he did, his defence'll claim he can't get a fair trial because of overblown and prejudicial newspaper coverage, then he'll be off the hook. We keep this to ourselves."

John would have enjoyed informing the press that he was making headway, but he couldn't jeopardize any future trial. It was a pity, because if the entire population had its eyes open for Ian Lowe, he wouldn't remain hidden for long. On top of that, John wouldn't have to suffer any more scathing editorial comments in newspapers, crucifying the team for lack of progress and referring to a meagre probationer in a high-profile position. Still, John had the skin of a rhinoceros. He would have to take yet more criticism before he arrested the Messenger.

From the parked car, Clare caught Greg's eye and signalled discreetly in Lance Golby's direction as he stopped his own car by the kerb outside his house. Greg nodded and set off, striding along the pavement. He needed to get his timing just right for Clare's test.

Lance clambered out of the car and picked up his

briefcase from the back seat. As he turned to walk towards his house, Greg burst into a run and crashed into him. Lance uttered a yelp of surprise, staggered and grabbed the garden hedge to stop himself from falling over. His briefcase clattered to the pavement.

"Sorry, mate," Greg bawled. "In a hurry!" He ran off.

Lance shook his head angrily, rubbed his arm and cursed under his breath. He bent down and salvaged his briefcase from the paving stones.

Inside the unmarked car, Clare murmured, "Interesting."

Brett looked at her and asked, "Satisfied?"

She nodded. "I won't convince you or John, but that's not the reflexes of a martial arts expert. If he was, Greg would've come off worse. He certainly wouldn't have gone in for all that tottering. Balance is everything. For me, Lance is out of it. He's not the Messenger who kills with a single blow."

Clare was right, Brett was not convinced. But he had to admit that Lance Golby did not look like a confident killer. After that performance, he could not be a strong candidate.

As soon as Lance had disappeared into his house, Greg slipped into the back seat and Clare pulled away, saying, "Thanks, Greg. Great performance. You've just bumped off one suspect."

"Anna Stimpson next?"

"Yeah," Clare replied, "if we can find her."

But they couldn't. Anna was working away in

Manchester. Clare could not put her through the same sly test.

It was an exceptionally low tide at King's Lynn. The level of water in the Great Ouse dropped so much that the rusting roof of a car appeared just above the waterline. Two observant beat officers from the Norfolk Constabulary reported the sighting. Within half an hour, divers were exploring the wreck. They identified it as Ian Lowe's car but no one was trapped inside. By the time of the next low tide, twelve hours later, there was a crane positioned alongside the river, its jib extending over the submerged vehicle. With sturdy cables attached to the car, the arm heaved it from the river. Water gushed from the dangling car like a sponge plucked from the water and squeezed by a giant hand.

On the bank a transporter waited to take the find back to the laboratory. Beside it, Big John Macfarlane watched and then, nodding at the sodden vehicle, ordered, "Take it apart. I want to know if there's anything in there that'll link it to any of our murders."

The forensic technician sighed. "You'll be lucky! Anything useful will have been—"

Interrupting, John said, "I'm well aware of the effects of water. But I don't care how unlikely it is, I want you to give it a go. We won't know for sure till you've gone over every millimetre of it. All right?"

The grumpy scientist mumbled, "Yeah. Sure. We'll do what we can."

The whereabouts of the car's owner remained a complete mystery.

No one was surprised when Umut died. After all, he was three years short of his century. For the last five years he had been little more than a bag of bones that moved stiffly and awkwardly. His friends and family loved him for his kindness but they had to admit that his death was inevitable and imminent. Yet, when he was found lifeless on the morning of Tuesday 27th February, his doctor was immediately suspicious. Umut was lying on his bed, face up. It looked like rapid death from cardiac arrest but there was a slight bruise on his cheek. Inside his mouth there was bruising where his lips had been pressed hard against his remaining teeth. One of his pillows lay on the floor beside his bed. And that wasn't all. The silver crucifix that hung constantly from his withered neck had gone. Besides, normal death did not leave a yellow visiting card. Umut had been smothered with his pillow. He had managed to live for ninety-seven years without harming anyone. Now, for some senseless and inexplicable reason, someone had harmed him.

He lived in Beeston, sandwiched between Nottingham and Junction 25 of the M1. His house was by the golf course, where the railway, Attenborough Nature Reserve and the River Trent met. It was five miles west of the steeplechase course at Colwick Park. There was no doubt: the killing had all of the Messenger's hallmarks. Umut was his ninth victim, his third indoor murder. And the wayward Messenger had broken one of Salma's general rules: apparently, serial killers did not always murder people with the same skin colour.

The Messenger's last three acts threatened to shatter the morale of Big John's team. A defenceless six-year-old girl, a fit man despatched with an unbelievably savage kick, and a vulnerable ninety-seven-year-old man. What had the detectives got to show for it? Ian Lowe's car but no sign of the unstable man himself. Nothing in the way of evidence from his watery vehicle. No significant new clues from Nottingham. And the chilling message from Umut's bedside cabinet – *By the time I have finished, everyone will know who I am* – written with letters and words cut from *The Sporting Life* and *Motoring News*. The team had reached its lowest ebb.

Brett called Greta in Forensics. "I've been thinking about these calling cards. No prints on them, probably because he wore gloves when he made them. But what about other traces? The glue he used on the back of the letters and words. Unless he did it in a sterile, dust-free room, surely there'd be some traces from his work area getting stuck in the glue. It'd end up between the back of the clippings and the card. Maybe the odd fibre or hair or something. Anything that might throw some light on him or the place where he glued the words on to the page."

"There speaks a desperate man?"

"Absolutely. Desperate for more facts, more evidence. The boss might get it from analysing human behaviour. I get it from you, analysing the scene of the crime."

"OK, I'll do what I can," Greta promised.

On 6th March, the Messenger departed from his MO again. Another new twist. Another jibe. When Mrs Shuttleworth got home from her shopping spree in Nuneaton she found a yellow card among her purchases. "What's this?" she mumbled to herself. Her face creased as she read the message, made up from words cut out of newspapers.

i could *have* killLED you. EASY. but no. LAW less neEDs a BREAK

"Well I never!" she exclaimed aloud. "How strange." With a frown she walked over to the bin and dropped it in. "Kids!" she muttered. Two minutes later, though, she returned to the waste bin, bent down and plucked it out again. "I don't know..." she mumbled to herself. She read the message again and then made up her mind. She went to the phone and called the police.

It was ironic, Brett thought, as he listened to Mrs Shuttleworth relate her trip into the town centre, that she would have had more to offer the investigation if the Messenger had carried out his threat. As long as he kept murdering there was a chance he'd slip up and leave a clue. He didn't wish murder on anyone but, as it was, Mrs Shuttleworth had nothing to give but the calling card and a list of the shops and streets that she had visited. With Clare, he'd get all of the videos from the security cameras in the area but there would be too many for a quick result. And he doubted that the Messenger would be so careless that he'd be caught by video surveillance, slipping his calling card into her shopping bag.

Mrs Shuttleworth seemed to be pleased to have an audience and so she wittered on. "What with all this on the telly these days, you're not safe anywhere, any time, are you? I didn't think at first. Well, you don't, do you? But you never know. With that horrid man doing... Ugh!" She shivered. "So I called. Just in case. It wasn't like this in my day, you know. We never used to lock up. We didn't have to. Friends could come and go. You could trust people in those days, you see. Now, well, you can't be sure who your friends are. You can be murdered in your own bed."

She was right. Umut had been murdered in his own bed. Who knows where Mrs Shuttleworth was when she could have been murdered by the Messenger?

The elderly woman could not get used to the idea of a female detective. She asked Clare, "Are you sure you're a policeman?"

"No," Clare answered, trying to maintain a patient smile, "I'm a police *officer*. A detective sergeant."

"Doesn't seem to me to be a job for… Anyway, what do you think, my dear?" she continued. "Is this card important?"

Clare shrugged. "We'll treat it seriously. Look into it. But I imagine it's just kids messing about."

"That's what I thought," Mrs Shuttleworth responded at once. "Kids! We were never like that, not when I was a youngster. In my day we had pranks. I'm not saying we didn't, but we didn't have all this mugging and housebreaking and taking cars. That's because in my day if you got into trouble you'd get a good hiding. You wouldn't do it again after a good hiding, I can tell you! And there's something else. Winters were never as bitter cold and miserable as this…"

Clare was speculating about the Messenger. If he had killed Mrs Shuttleworth, surely he'd have removed her tongue.

Brett and Clare excused themselves as soon as they could. Once they'd escaped Mrs Shuttleworth's ceaseless chatter, they headed for the town to commandeer all of the relevant video material from the private security companies that spied on central Nuneaton and its shops.

Back in Sheffield, the incident room was thinning. Brett put a fresh drawing pin in the map, just by Nuneaton. Like the pin over Luton, it was green. There were nine red drawing pins, marking the murder sites, and the two green ones depicting near misses. He took an enlarged copy of the Nuneaton message and stuck it on the wall with the others.

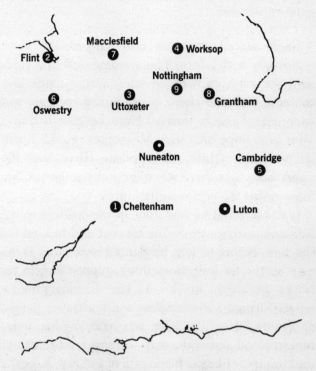

Brett's eyes flitted from the map to the catalogue of mementoes to the list of messages. It was infuriating. He knew that he should be seeing a pattern but nothing jumped out at him. He scanned the messages and picked out the strange ones that perhaps held a hidden meaning rather than simply declaring the Messenger's wish to be famous or making jokes about Brett's name.

I am complete.
I've got to go now – to the top of a...
End of the line.

Brett stared at them and tapped the desk
repeatedly with a biro. The messages left him cold.
And the message with his latest victim made him
colder still: *By the time I have finished, everyone will
know who I am.* It worried Brett because it didn't
offer any hope that the Messenger would finish
killing soon. Quite the opposite. Brett got the
impression that there was a long way to go yet. He
flung down the biro in agitation.

It was late and he was alone in the incident room.
Still annoyed, he threw on his coat and headed for
the door. Before he left, he glanced once more at the
map on the far wall. Something stopped him in his
tracks. Suddenly, he saw it. The drawing pins no
longer formed a meaningless and frustrating tangle
of coloured dots. The killer was scrawling his signa-
ture in blood across the map – across the breadth of
the country – like the inane grin of a clown. Like the
despicable cruel smile of the complete psychotic. *By
the time I have finished, everyone will know who I am.*

"Yes!" Brett's spine tingled and he pointed a
finger at the map and exclaimed, "Got you!"

Leaving a half-drunk mug of coffee, he murmured
to himself, "At last." It was the moment he'd been
waiting for. The moment when the killings made

perverse sense. And it *was* obvious. He punched Clare's number into the telephone and waited. "Come on," he muttered impatiently, urging his partner to respond to the ringing. He knew that he should be calling John Macfarlane at his hotel, but first he wanted to share his discovery with Clare.

When Clare walked into the bar, it was nearly eleven o'clock. "I hope this is important, Brett," she said. "I was tucked up with Yevtushenko."

"Yevtushenko?"

"Russian poet. Fearless spokesman of his generation in the nineteen fifties and sixties."

"You collect poets like I collect fish," Brett noted with a smile.

Clare looked at him and, suddenly serious, said, "You've cracked it, haven't you? You're looking happier tonight than you have for months. You know who the Messenger is!"

Brett nodded. "I'll get you a drink. You have a look at that." He gave her a sketch of the country, marked with the locations of the murders and the incidents near Luton and Nuneaton.

When he returned with her pint, he asked, "Seen it yet?"

"Seen what?"

"It's like one of those Magic Eye pictures. You don't see the real picture for ages then, in a flash, it's totally obvious."

"Is it?" she said, tilting the map to a different angle.

"Well, OK, think of it as a join-the-dots puzzle. Join Flint and Oswestry and what have you got?"

"One," Clare replied. "Or an I."

"Exactly. Capital I. What did the Oswestry calling card say? *I am complete*. It should have been *I is complete*. The letter I is complete."

Excited, Clare muttered, "I see what you mean. But what are Uttoxeter and Macclesfield then?"

"Halfway to making a capital A. Macclesfield's at the top."

"Are you sure?" Clare checked. "It's not just a coincidence? An optical illusion."

"No. I'm sure," Brett answered. "What did the Messenger say to *The Sheffield Gazette* editor on the phone, just before his little jaunt to Macclesfield? He said, 'I've got to go now, to the top of a...' The editor reckoned he'd been cut off but he hadn't. There's no missing word. It was just, 'I've got to go to the top of A'." Triumphantly, Brett declared, "Macclesfield *is* the top of an A."

"Nottingham, Worksop and Grantham form most of an N, then," Clare surmised.

"Spot on. And remember the Grantham message?

End of the line. It's literally true. End of the line that spells IAN."

"Brilliant work, Brett!" Clare congratulated him. "It *is* obvious. Written right across the map. But what about underneath? Cheltenham, Nuneaton, Luton and Cambridge? It's not so obvious."

"No," Brett admitted. "It's early days, but he might be planning an L in Wales. Cheltenham and Nuneaton could be part of an O. If Luton's part of his game, it'll probably be in a W and Cambridge's part of an E, no doubt. Ian Lowe's our man. *By the time I've finished, everyone will know who I am*. He's giving the whole country his autograph. At the end, he'd invite us all to join the dots. I hate to admit that the profiler was right, but she said he'd want to get caught in the end. The ultimate fame, she called it, when everyone finds out who he is."

"So," Clare said, "all that about horse-racing, golf courses, railways and rivers was just … irrelevant."

"Pure coincidence," Brett stated, "or a deliberate attempt to lead us astray. Either way, it adds up to nothing."

"Ian Lowe," Clare whispered. "It all fits." In the light of Brett's insight, she shelved her reservations about Ian Lowe's ability to deliver the blow that killed a man in Grantham. "All we've got to do now is catch him."

"Yeah," Brett agreed, his smile fading.

"Have you been in touch with the boss?" asked Clare.

"No. I wanted to test it on you before I disturb him at this time of night."

Clare nodded. "Well," she said, finishing her drink, "I think it's time to go and break the news."

"You don't want to go back to Yevtushenko?"

"Yes. But I'll come and keep you company."

"Thanks," Brett replied.

Big John was still sitting in the hotel bar, its last customer. He was ignoring all of the staff's hints as they cleaned up all around him. He squinted sceptically at the map. "Ian Lowe?" he mumbled. He tilted his head quizzically and then announced, "I see what you mean. Ian Lowe."

"The victims *were* chosen at random but the locations weren't," Brett concluded.

"Good work," John proclaimed. Unable to resist teasing Brett, he added, "So, it didn't come down to forensic data, analysis of newspaper print, or anything like that. It came down to understanding what he was up to, what was in his brain when he decided to kill. Surprise, surprise!" John's elation at Brett's discovery didn't last long. "Unfortunately, though, we can't just go out and arrest him. We haven't got a clue where he is. Get the night shift to post some cops at his house, Brett. Twenty-four-hour watch from now on." He stopped for air and beer, then continued, "We're not really one step in front of him, either, are we? There's too many possible sites for his next strike. We can't saturate the target areas with beat officers."

"No. He's not writing his name in the right order. We don't know which letter he'll work on next. We'd only be able to guess his next location when there's only one or two dots needed to complete his name."

"And that's far too late," John responded. "We need to find him now. Or at least tomorrow."

First thing in the morning, Big John allowed Brett to break the news of his revelation to the squad. Then John called for suggestions on how to find Ian Lowe.

"There's always the public," Greg called out. "That's the best way."

"No." John was adamant that to reveal their prime suspect to the press could risk the case against him. "I won't— Hang on." He made for the telephone, mumbling something about the chief constable in any force that, so far, had not been blighted by the Messenger.

Later that day, when the national news was broadcast, a call was put out by Northamptonshire Police for a man called Ian Lowe. His picture was displayed in close-up while the police spokesperson explained that, following a mix-up at a pharmacy, Mr Lowe might be in possession of medication that could seriously harm him. It was vital that Ian should go to his nearest police station immediately or, if seen by members of the public, his whereabouts should be reported at once. It was stressed that the photograph was not up-to-date. Ian would look a little older and he might have grown a moustache, for example. The news item was neat and believable: nothing to do with a series of brutal crimes, nothing to do with the team investigating the Messenger, nothing to jeopardize his prosecution for multiple murder.

Following the broadcast, Ian Lowe himself did not come forward, of course, but he was reported to have been seen by people throughout the country. Supposed sightings came in from Northern Ireland to Yarmouth, Exeter to Aberdeen. Big John had more phones installed so that he and his team could deal with each possibility. Ardently, he persuaded each busy local force to find the resource to follow up the reports without delay.

Amid the feverish activity, Clare gazed at the large map on the wall and then prodded Brett. "What would you say if the Messenger killed someone here?" she asked, jumping up and pointing to a spot just to the east of Oswestry. "A small place called Wem," she added as she scanned the map.

"Bottom left of the A of IAN," Brett replied.

"Mmm." Clare hesitated and then said, "Not forming an L with Flint and Oswestry?"

"What are you saying?" Brett queried.

She traced out the letters. "L here, then the A and N as before. Underneath, Nuneaton and Cheltenham could be part of a giant C and Luton and Cambridge part of a capital E."

"Lance?" Brett hesitated, unsure of himself. For an instant, he went cold. In that moment he thought that he might have misled everyone. If he was wrong, the investigation was going off at a tangent and wasting time, energy and money. Then he remembered something. "No, it can't be," he said with relief. "*I am complete*. He wouldn't have come up with that unless the first letter is I."

"Ah, yes," Clare responded, sitting down again. "You've got a point there. Forget it."

"Besides, I thought you'd discounted him because he didn't pass your shoulder-barge test."

"I know," Clare answered. "I'm just thinking through all the possibilities."

By Wednesday 14th March, almost all of the notified sightings had been checked out and dismissed. Each reported person had been traced and, because of a passing resemblance to Ian Lowe, had been found to be a case of mistaken identity. A few sightings had drawn a blank and remained an enigma. On his next killing day, Ian Lowe was still at large. The team's optimism had evaporated once more.

On the banks of the Avon, in the recreation ground opposite the Royal Shakespeare Theatre, the Messenger went about his grisly business as usual. The woman didn't matter as a person. She was important only as a vessel for his next message to Lawless. Her destiny was to become a point on a map. In that, she was vital to the Messenger. For that, she had to die. He believed that his requirement for her body was paramount, much greater than anyone else's need for this woman alive. She should be honoured, privileged to be part of his plan.

First thing in the morning, it was Liz who alerted them to developments in Stratford. The bleak news arrived at her computer like a hammer blow.

"Stratford!" Brett cried. "But that's…" He strode to the map and picked out its location. "It's on a direct line between Cheltenham and Nuneaton."

"So?"

He placed the red-headed drawing pin in Stratford and stood back. "That can't be part of an O." He paused for the implication to sink in. "Lowe just doesn't fit any more."

John groaned aloud. "Well, we can't bring in everyone called Ian for questioning."

"It's worse than that, Boss," Greg put in. "It might not be *Ian*. It could be *I am*, with a word below still to come."

John slumped into a seat. "This is getting ridiculous. At one moment we know his name, we've almost got him. At the next, we're back where we started. It could be anyone and we're waiting for him to come up with a description of himself. I am … happy? I am … enjoying myself? I am … walking all over the police."

"Whatever he is," Brett responded, "I'm still sure it's a name. Remember, *By the time I have finished, everyone will know who I am* and *She will help me make a name for myself*. He's making a name!" Brett stressed heatedly. "He wants his name to be known – eventually. His profile tells us that. His own messages tell us. Whatever he's spelling out, his name's in there. I think it *is* Ian."

"Yes," John said. "Or it's your imagination in serious overdrive, running away with you. And us following behind."

still flounder ING, lawless ?

Big John sighed when he read the note. "Not exactly helpful, just an insult." He shrugged and murmured, "At least I don't need forensics to tell me where the *flounder* came from. *Angling Times* again, I bet."

Brett tried to manage a smile. In the aftermath of murder, it was difficult.

They were standing in the pleasant parkland near the Royal Shakespeare Theatre but on the other side of the river. One of Anna Stimpson's haunts, as Clare pointed out.

The local CID officer said, "We've got you a witness – of sorts. A Rodney Haycock. You'll find him over at the theatre. He's an actor."

"OK," John replied. "We'll go and have a chat with him."

Directed past the posters advertising the production of *King Lear*, they found the great man in a rest room. John began by asking him why he'd been out walking through the park so late at night.

"I am an actor," he announced pompously. "I am Lear. During the day I'm recognized by autograph hunters and the like, so I tend to take my air at night. Besides, I find a solitary walk in the dark most enriching. Little did I know that last night..." He hesitated.

"'Twas a naughty night to swim in,'" Clare quoted.

Rodney opened his mouth and exclaimed, "You know *King Lear*!"

"'Ay, my good lord.'"

"'So young, and so untender?'" he enunciated loudly as if addressing a distant audience.

"'So young, my lord, and true.'"

Rodney's enthusiastic laugh could have knocked them backwards. "Excellent! A policewoman with style and culture."

Brett and John watched with raised eyebrows.

Having buttered up the actor, Clare asked, "Can you tell us about last night? What exactly did you see?"

"Not a great deal, I'm afraid. It was rather like a distant stage. A dark scene. *Macbeth*, perhaps. But no. It was *this* great stage of fools," he said fancifully, spreading his arms to indicate the real world. "I saw the lady strolling by the river. Her form and poise suggested elegance and contentment. She was wearing a hood or headscarf. I saw her approached by a man. All just silhouettes, you understand." He was ignoring John and Brett and directing his comments solely to Clare, gazing steadily into her face as he spoke. "I assumed it was a midnight tryst. Lovers! Romance! But then," he recounted in a whisper, "the man drew out something. I understand from the other officer that it was a knife. He must have plunged it cruelly into her. I saw only what seemed to be an arm reaching out for her. But then she dropped and I knew."

"What did the man do?"

"He bent down and whisked something – a headscarf, I think – from the poor unfortunate woman. Then he ran very swiftly back towards the road."

"Was it definitely a man?"

"Oh, I can't say. You should know better than to ask that of one in the theatre. How many times have I seen women effective in the role of men?"

Clare extracted from him the best description of the Messenger that she could but it added nothing to previous versions. Finally she enquired, "Do you know Anna Stimpson, theatrical agent?"

"Indeed," he answered. "My daughter, Cordelia, is one of her clients."

To check, John interjected, "That's a daughter in the play?"

"Of course," Rodney replied, as if he were talking to a fool.

"Have you seen her – Anna Stimpson?" Clare asked.

"No, but Cordelia told me she was in the audience last night. Anna had come to watch her client, apparently."

"OK," Clare said. "Thanks for your help."

"Pleasure," Rodney returned with gusto. "You have brightened my otherwise troubled day. 'The gods to their dear shelter take thee, maid.'"

On their way out of the theatre, Brett nudged Clare. "Phew!" he said. "I thought for a moment he'd offer you a part and keep you in there."

"He couldn't afford the transfer fee," Clare replied with a grin.

John chipped in, "You handled him well, Clare, but he didn't exactly add to our picture of the Messenger."

"No," Clare confessed, "but now we know Anna Stimpson was here last night."

In the car, Greta called Brett on his mobile phone. "Remember you asked me to take a good look behind the newspaper clippings for anything adhering to the glue?" she asked.

"Yes," Brett replied optimistically, questioningly.

"Well, when you get back here, come on down and take a look for yourself. But don't get overexcited – I haven't got much."

While Clare went with John to interview Anna Stimpson, Brett hurried to Greta's familiar domain.

He felt at home among the samples and scientific instruments.

"Take a look," Greta invited, waving him towards a microscope. "I've mounted a couple of finds from one card on the same slide. There are several others like them on the other cards."

Brett found himself peering at two opaque and jagged patches like crystals of ice. They were criss-crossed with fine lines like netting. "What are they?" he asked.

"Skin," Greta announced succinctly. "Human skin."

"Interesting," Brett declared. "Where from? Household dust?"

"Possibly, but they're a bit big for that."

"They couldn't come off his fingers," Brett reasoned, "because we think he was wearing gloves."

"So…" Greta prompted to see if he would come to the same conclusion that she had already reached.

"I'm not sure."

"How would he work?" Greta prompted. "Think of making up one of these cards yourself."

Brett sat on the bench, pulled a piece of paper towards himself and, head down, began to fiddle with it as if he were cutting and pasting. He glanced up at Greta blankly, carried on the pretence for a few seconds and then scratched his head. Abruptly, his finger froze in his hair and he jumped up again. "I see what you mean," he said animatedly. "That's brilliant!"

"Really? I wouldn't go that far. It only tells you—"

"It's enough," he interrupted in his excitement. "Combined with everything else I didn't understand – like the Ecstasy and the Stratford murder – it tells me everything!" He headed for the exit, pausing at the door to call, "You're a treasure, Greta. Where would I be without you?"

"Up a certain creek, I expect."

Back in the incident room, Brett took a long look at the map with its extra drawing pin at Stratford and then leaned over Liz, asking, "Can you get me a list of all the Nottinghamshire personnel who took part in the drugs raid on Mixers, ninth of January? Their full names."

Liz frowned. "I guess so, if their Drug Squad is still talking to us. Why?"

"I'd rather not say yet," Brett answered. "Too much like tempting fate. But it might be the key to the whole thing. Just trust me. Drop everything to find out."

"All right," she replied. "No skin off my nose."

Brett smiled. "That's true. I think it came from somewhere else entirely."

"You what?"

"Sorry, Liz," he said. "Forget it. Just my warped sense of humour."

"Very warped."

Brett got himself a mug of coffee and sipped it distractedly as he waited. One of the Messenger's sentences had been bothering him, swirling around his brain like a cloying song. *Maybe I should be called Lawless instead*. "Instead of what?" Brett had asked himself. Now he thought that he knew. Now it slotted into the jigsaw like the flakes of skin, the drug on the coat sleeve, and the killing in Stratford. Suddenly his elation waned. It struck him that, if he'd solved the crime, there was little cause for jubilation. His theory was too appalling to be relished. He wanted the information from the raid on Mixers to provide a definite answer – to put a stop to the Messenger – but he dreaded it as well. He believed that Liz was about to confirm his new theory and yet it was so shocking that, in a way, he would have preferred her to demolish it. He wanted to be wrong.

His mixed feelings were interrupted by Liz's shout. "Thanks to the miracle of electronic communication, I'm on-line to someone with the knowledge and authority to release the details you want, but he's turning awkard. Wants to know why you need the information. Another outbreak of divisional rivalry, I guess."

"What rank is he?"

Liz smiled. "You can't pull rank. He's at inspector level. Probably a proper one, not like you."

"Very funny," Brett retorted without returning her grin. "But John's not here to throw his weight around..." He hesitated and then said, "Tell him it's just that we may need to get permission to interview their crew to find out some details about our victim who may have been in Mixers that night. That should do it."

It did. The Nottinghamshire officer seemed to be satisfied with Brett's artful reason and a list of officers and uniformed backup appeared on Liz's computer.

Immediately, Brett scrolled down the list to see the catalogue of backup that the Nottinghamshire Constabulary had used. A short-lived smile appeared on his face. He tapped the screen at one particular name and uttered, "That's the answer." He looked upwards and let out a long breath. It suggested both relief and anger. "Phone John, will you? Get him back straightaway. It doesn't matter what he's doing, just get him back. There's some delicate negotiation to do and it'll take someone of his authority to do it."

"Don't you want to do it?"

"No. I've got a delicate call to take care of myself. I need to call the duty officer at Worksop. I've got to find an excuse for luring Constable Louise Jenson out of her home territory."

"Yeah," Big John said heatedly, mopping his forehead. "I see the map. I see what you mean."

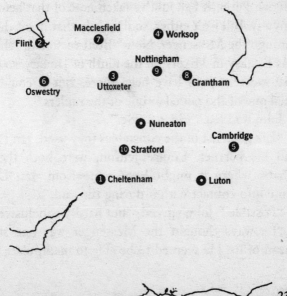

Macclesfield
7

Flint
2

Worksop
4

Nottingham
9

Grantham
8

Oswestry
6

Uttoxeter
3

Nuneaton

Cambridge
5

Stratford
10

Cheltenham
1

Luton

He continued, "But if you want to arrest a police constable from a neighbouring force, you need a watertight case – or all hell will break loose. It'll have to be good even to get me to withdraw the watch from Ian Lowe's house. So, persuade me that you're right. And I don't want to hear about the writing on the map. A little while ago, according to you, it proved Lowe was our man. Now it says something else. I think you'd better convince me without it."

Brett sighed. "It might be tricky without the map but I'll try. First, though, let me say I never knew Constable Law's first name. Liz found out it's Ian. Ian Law matches the map precisely. But forgetting that for a moment, how come the Messenger's coat had Ecstasy on its sleeve? Ian Lowe isn't exactly a party animal. Perhaps I should've taken note of that before. Anyway, Bill isn't either, so it's likely that it got there through the Messenger. Now," Brett reasoned, "there was Ecstasy in Mixers on the ninth of January, so the coat wearer could have been there. But it could've been one of the raided *or* one of the raiders."

John nodded. "Good angle."

"Liz got a list of the constables they used. Ian Law and his partner, Louise Jenson, were both there. That's where it might have come from. Ian Law came into contact with it during the raid."

"Possible," John agreed, "but hardly conclusive."

"I always thought the Messenger was one step ahead of us. He seemed to be able to manipulate us, guess what we'd deduce from each killing. That suggests he knew our thinking. Quite reasonable for a police officer. And that's how come he managed to leave so few clues. He knows our procedures." Brett paused and then continued, "One of his messages was, *Maybe I should be called Lawless instead*. This was a bigger hint than I thought. I think it means, maybe *he* should be called Lawless instead of me – or instead of his own name. In other words, maybe I should be Law and *he* should be Lawless."

"Is that it?" John enquired, unimpressed.

Clare chipped in, "Didn't that medium talk about the Messenger living a lie? There's no bigger lie than living the life of a policeman *and* being a murderer."

"True." With sarcasm John said, "I'll phone Notts and say we want to arrest one of their boys because a fortune-teller told us so."

"There's something else," Brett mentioned. "Behind some of the letters on his calling cards, there are several pieces of skin. Where did they come from? I noticed, when I first met Constable Law, that he suffers from dandruff. When he makes up the calling cards at a desk or whatever, some flakes of skin are going to fall into the glue."

"And can Greta tell us it's *his* skin?"

"No," Brett confessed.

"Then I can't authorize his arrest," John stated firmly.

"I know," Brett said. "None of these things is absolutely conclusive but they all point in the same direction. They all add up. And there's the evidence of the map."

"If he *is* spelling out his name, it's not yet fully formed so it's open to interpretation. Apparently, we've got it wrong once already."

"That's why I took the decision to interview his partner, Louise Jenson," Brett declared. "That'll sort it out one way or the other. She's on her way."

"And, if she spoke to Law, won't it alert him that you're on to him?"

"I don't think so," Brett answered. "You see, when she left, she thought her parents had had an accident over here. Since then I've spoken to her in her car on her mobile, apologized for the deception and told her we need some vital information from her about the Nicola Morrison case."

"Good," John replied. "I want to be in on this … chat, but I want you and Clare to handle it. You got us this far. She's your witness. If you're right, you deserve the credit. If you're wrong," he added wryly, "your head's on the chopping block."

Brett, Clare and John waited in silence with the same thoughts in their heads. They were sickened by the notion of an upholder of the law turned killer. They were apprehensive about the prospect of arresting a fellow officer. They knew that their colleagues in Nottinghamshire would not easily be persuaded of Law's guilt. The Notts brigade would stick up for one of its own until the evidence was undeniable. John's team would be regarded as troublemakers and intruders in their own affairs. If Ian Law was the Messenger, his arrest would be harrowing.

The formalities could wait. If there had to be a recorded interview, then it could happen later. For now, Brett, Clare and John escorted Louise to a spare office where they could talk informally. The young recruit was visibly tense. She did not have to be told that there was more at stake than a question or two about the discovery of Nicola Morrison's body.

"Have a seat," Brett offered.

"What is this?" she stammered as she sat down. Her worried expression suggested that she believed she was on trial. "Have I done something wrong?"

"Not at all," Clare answered, taking the lead. "We just need to ask you some questions. And we needed you away from Notts before we could tell you the real reason. First, though, we need to check your relationship with Constable Law." Clare wanted to start by establishing Louise's loyalties. "In the police force it's all about teamwork. I'm sure you've discovered that already. And teams acquire a life of their own – a comradeship, if you like. Partnerships develop. That's good. It works. The relationship that builds between partners is important, but there's a more important allegiance: an allegiance to the law itself. Do you see what I mean, and do you agree with it?"

Louise maintained a frown because she was uncertain about what was coming next, but she said, "Yes, of course."

"How would you describe your relationship with Ian?"

"Um... Businesslike. He's been very helpful. Guided me past the worst pitfalls, I think. I'm grateful to him."

"Would you call him a friend?"

Louise hesitated. "A good colleague, yes. But a friend? I, er, I'm not sure. He's ... I don't know ... a bit distant for that, I suppose. Why?"

"I've got to know that you'll be truthful above anything else, even above your allegiance to a colleague," Clare explained. "When we ask you about Ian – which we've got to do – you will be honest with us, won't you, Louise?"

Stressed, Louise nodded nervously.

"OK. Good." Clare paused as the door opened and then said, "Ah, coffees all round! That's what we need. Thanks, Greg." Once they had all taken a polystyrene cup of piping hot coffee, Clare resumed. "Bearing in mind what we've just said about loyalties, have you ever noticed anything odd about Ian Law's behaviour?"

"Odd?"

"For instance, would you say he's happy in the police force?"

"Oh, yes," Louise gushed. She paused for a moment and then added, "Or rather, he would be. I suppose I ought to say he's got a huge chip on his shoulder. He loves the job but reckons he's always passed over when it comes to promotion. It's always a younger person who gets the credit, he's said lots of times. He thinks he's invisible to the boss. Once he said…" She stopped and looked at Brett sheepishly.

"Go on," Brett prompted. "This is very important. You can be open with us."

"Well, he's talked about you," she admitted, glancing at Brett. "Said you looked too young for a detective inspector. He asked around about you – did quite a bit of research on you, I think – then grumbled that you didn't have any experience but you landed a top job just because you went to university." Her cheeks were bright pink.

To relax Louise, Brett smiled and murmured, "He's not the first to think that. He's right as well."

"He said you weren't getting anywhere with this serial murder case. He reckoned he'd do much better if only the powers-that-be would give him the chance."

Brett wondered if he had finally fathomed what the killings were all about. If Ian Law was the Messenger, he'd murdered to embarrass Brett – to confirm his criticism of someone who had used Graduate Entry to the force and climbed up the ladder very quickly. Ian, still in uniform at twice Brett's age, was trying to prove his superiority over Brett – a mere constable outwitting a detective inspector. Ian had been overlooked by his superiors and he didn't want to be overlooked any more. As they didn't heed his good work, he'd become famous for the opposite.

To confirm Brett's thoughts, Louise added, "I

remember once he said, 'One day the Chief will notice me. I'll make sure of that.' He was really determined. I thought he meant he'd make some really cracking arrests." She paused before deducing, "But, because you're asking me these things, perhaps it meant something else. Why are you…?"

"Just bear with us a minute, Louise," Clare interrupted. "Do you know if he went in for keep-fit, maybe through martial arts?"

Louise nodded. "Oh, yes. For his age, he's ever so fit. He prides himself on it. Always working out. I always felt safe on duty with him. He's a class act when it comes to karate. He's in the Notts Police club."

"All right," Clare said, with a glance at her own partner. "I see you've brought your logbook along. I want you to tell us your days off since Christmas. Let's start with Christmas Eve."

Louise put down her coffee and opened her diary. Flicking through its pages, she listed all of the dates when she was not at work. One-by-one, she reeled them off and, as she did so, she sensed the growing tension in the room. The dates included every one of the Messenger's strike days except 17th January and 12th February.

Immediately, Brett queried, "Did Ian have the same days off?"

"Yes. Our schedules are the same."

Ian Law would not have needed a day off work to kill Nicola Morrison in Worksop in January. But if he was on duty in Nottinghamshire on the afternoon of 12th February, he could not have committed a murder in Macclesfield. Clare looked anxiously at Brett before asking Louise, "You were at work on the twelfth of February. Was Ian as well, then?"

"Yes. We were on patrol in Worksop itself." To check her answer, she examined her notebook again and then murmured, "Oh, hang on. That day was different. I had a different partner. Ian was supposed to be on duty but he was off sick."

Not sick enough to stop him killing a six-year-old girl in Macclesfield. Or rather, he was sick enough to kill ten people just to be noticed.

"Louise," John put in, "I've heard all I need to hear. We've kept you in the dark long enough. You deserve an explanation now. I might as well be blunt. You see, what you've just told us confirms that your partner, Ian Law, is our serial killer."

Louise opened her mouth but nothing came out.

"I'm sorry," Brett told her. "But you see why we had to put you through this."

Still shocked, she gasped, "Yes."

"Where is he now?" Brett enquired.

Louise found it difficult to absorb Brett's question. Sluggishly, as if she had been stunned by a blow, she looked at her watch. "Sorry," she mumbled. "This is a real bombshell for me. I, er, he'll be … on duty. I'm not sure where. Sorry. But in half an hour he'll go to the canteen for a sandwich. At least, that's what he normally does."

Brett breathed in deeply. "Thanks, Louise. Thanks for being so candid with us. You'll make a good, honest police officer. For the moment, your bit's done. Take a break. Now, it's up to us to go and get him."

While Louise waited, ashen with shock, Big John drew Brett and Clare aside. He whispered, "All right, you've convinced me. What do you want to do now? Raid the canteen in a neighbouring force's police station?"

Brett nodded. "Straightaway. Before he strikes again."

John let out a long groan. "OK," he decided, "but it won't be easy. You two set out. Take Greg and Mark. I'll have to stay here and, while you're on the way, I'll try and clear it with the Chief Constable over there. Don't expect a huge amount of cooperation – no one likes meddlers. I'll sort out what I can for you but police forces aren't exactly known for appreciating raids on their own cops in their own station. Still, I'll do my best to get you some backup." He sniffed and concluded, "Go on. Hit the road. And remember, he's deadly with or without a weapon. Good luck."

Louise drove Brett and Greg in her own car while Clare and Mark travelled in another. During the journey, Brett asked more questions. "How many doors are there into your canteen, Louise?"

"Just the one," she said.

"I want to ask your opinion on something," Brett said, "or perhaps I should say, put a proposition to you. Just say no if you don't fancy it. You see, I don't want a big confrontation. You could go in to the canteen and join your partner – all quite normal. Just chat with him like you usually do. Put him at ease. But you make sure you stand between him and the door, blocking off the view. You see, I don't want him to see us coming in. That way, we take him by surprise. We stand a chance of a smooth arrest and no casualties if we don't give him any warning."

"Do I have to? Are you ordering me to do it?" Louise asked. "You see, it's hard for me to take it in. I can hardly believe that the man who's helped me so much is a multiple murderer. A little strange, yes, but... It'd be like betraying him."

"I understand," Brett responded. "I can't order you to do anything. You don't work for me, but even if you did, I wouldn't order you to do it anyway. It's got to be your decision. He's a fighter so there's an element of danger."

Louise lapsed into silence for a few seconds. Then she made up her mind. "Yes. I'm supposed to be a professional. Of course I'll do it." She was dreading it but she was not short on courage.

"Good. Thanks, Louise."

Bleakly, Greg chipped in, "I'm just not sure four of us will be enough, Brett. From what I've seen, he could despatch four people pretty easily."

"That's why I want the element of surprise. And I'm hoping John will wangle enough backup from Notts to make it impossible for him to escape. They might even come up with an armed response. Don't forget Clare, though. I don't want us to get into a fight but, if we do, Clare may be a match for him."

"Risky," Greg muttered.

"We're trying to take a violent and intelligent serial killer, Greg. Risk is part of the deal, I'm afraid."

Before long, John called Brett on his mobile phone. "You've got a bit of cooperation, but not much assistance," he announced. "You'll be met at the door and escorted to the canteen. That's about it. No extra troops. Ian Law's just taken up residence, apparently, but Nottinghamshire won't tackle him themselves. If you ask me, they don't want to put any of their own officers in the firing line for an investigation that's not theirs. And, of course, they haven't seen the evidence. But once you're in the building, they'll seal it to stop him getting out. The Chief Constable's not going to authorize an armed response. Not a hope. Not in a police station where the suspect's surrounded by coppers. He can't see the need. I must say I sympathize. You know me and guns – dreadful things, best avoided. I should think you agree after Upper Needless."

"Yes, I do," Brett answered. The last time that he had been involved with firearms, he'd felt the cold barrel of a loaded gun against his own temple and his girlfriend had not survived. "Thanks for your help. I'll take it from here."

"Keep me informed," John commanded him.

At the door of Worksop Police Station, Louise nodded respectfully at the waiting officer, Detective Chief Inspector Halford. "Come on," he said tersely to the small delegation from South Yorkshire. "You can come in on my warrant card. And," he said to Louise, "thank you, Constable Jenson. You can take up your normal duties now."

"But…" She looked at Brett.

On the way in, Brett explained that he had planned to use Louise.

"And you've agreed to this?" Halford checked with his constable. He was surprised by her compliance.

She nodded. "Yes."

"So be it," he replied hastily. He was not prepared either to commend or overrule her decision. "I'm sure you appreciate the risk – if Ian Law's guilty – but if you're prepared…"

The group strode down the corridor, enduring the puzzled frowns of passing local officers, and stopped short of the canteen. "It's there. Next door on the right," Halford informed them coldly.

"Still willing to take it on?" Brett said to Louise.

She nodded as if she couldn't speak through nerves.

"All right," Brett said in a hushed voice. "Here's the plan. Louise goes in and blocks his line of sight, then I slip in unseen, followed by Clare."

Clare interrupted his flow, saying, "Shouldn't I go in first, just in case?"

"Very noble, Clare, but no. We act together. The idea is that you appear on one side of Louise and I appear on the other – at the same time."

"OK," Clare said. She asked Louise, "Is he right-handed or left?"

"Right, I think," she murmured.

"I'll take his more dangerous right side then, Brett. If he lashes out, I'm more likely to be able to fend it off."

"Agreed," Brett said. "Greg and Mark, you stay at the door. It's the only way out so, if he gets past me and Clare somehow, it's up to you to arrest him. But there's no need to risk yourselves. The building's locked up now, isn't it?" he asked Halford.

"As soon as you go in, it will be," he replied, scowling. He showed them a radiophone in his hand. "My Chief told me to put people at all exits to seal the place," he muttered without a trace of good grace.

"That's it, then," Brett concluded, disregarding Halford's hostility. "All ready? We've got him trapped, it seems. Let's get the job done quickly and smoothly. OK, Louise?" He touched her arm. "The first bit's up to you. Just act normally."

She didn't quite manage a smile or a confident response, but said in a faintly quivering voice, "I'm ready." She breathed in deeply and then walked the short distance down the corridor, turned and, without a backward glance, pushed her way into the canteen.

"One minute," Brett said. "We give her one minute to make sure she's in position, but not long enough for her to get into trouble with the topic of conversation. Then we go in."

They waited in silence, steeling themselves. Brett needed only to recall the young victims, Leanne and Jayne, to awaken his sense of outrage and resolve. Clare was still seething over the Grantham killing. Both Clare and Brett were determined to bring the Messenger's murderous regime to an end.

"Ready?" Brett asked his partner in a whisper.

In reply, she merely nodded.

"Let's go, then."

In the entrance to the canteen, Brett looked towards Louise. She was doing exactly what Brett had asked of her. From the doorway, they could see only her back as she stood, talking to someone who was sitting at a table on the far side of the room. Brett slipped into the canteen and Clare followed him. Quietly, they walked stealthily across the carpet, keeping Louise between them and Ian Law. At the last moment, Brett glanced behind him to receive Clare's acknowledgement. Together they moved, appearing on either side of the young constable. Brett glanced down at her mentor and began, "Ian Law, I am—"

Immediately, the policeman stood up and growled, "So, you've finally twigged. Took you long enough, Lawless. A bit slow for a detective inspector," he mocked.

"Turn round, Constable Law, and put your hands behind your back."

Ignoring him, Ian stared wildly at Louise and snapped, "Are you in on this? Was it you who shopped me? After all I've—"

Brett interrupted. "Turn round," he ordered again. "We've sealed the building. You can't—"

"Oh, yes I can!" Ian roared. Before Clare or Brett could react, his right arm flashed out and grabbed Louise. In an instant, he'd spun her round and pulled her to him. His forearm was pressed into her throat, stifling her scream. "You'll let me out or this traitor will be number eleven."

Louise's eyes bulged and her face was turning pink but she couldn't say anything.

"I'm perfectly capable of killing her right now – in front of you," Ian snorted.

Clare replied, "I'm well aware of that."

"Ah. You know these things." Ian eyed Clare closely and then said, "You're the danger, then, not Lawless."

Ignoring him, Brett said, "Take it easy. Don't harm her."

"Let me out, then I'll let her go."

"This won't do you any good, Ian. You know that."

"Move!" He tightened his grip and Louise lost the ability to breathe. She started to choke.

"Getting out won't help. I've got marksmen outside," Brett said.

Ian peered into Brett's eyes and said, "You're bluffing. Any second now, she'll pass out. Soon after, she's dead, Lawless."

Brett groaned, "All right." He stood aside.

Before moving, Ian scrutinized the people at the door and demanded, "Shift your gorillas and have the back exit unlocked."

Brett took one look at the distress on Louise's face and the developing distance in her eyes and nodded towards Greg, Mark and Halford. Brett's men moved out of the way and the local officer spoke urgently into his phone. "Done," he reported.

Ian relieved the pressure on Louise's throat and she began to gulp air again and cough. Not waiting for her to recover, he propelled her towards the corridor and freedom.

Helpless, Brett and Clare watched them go.

At the door, Ian called over his shouler, "Nice try, Lawless, but you'll have to do better than that. See you soon. Very soon. Without her," he said inclining his head towards Clare. "Keep her on a leash." As a parting shot, he added, "Don't try and follow me or I twist this arm and her neck snaps."

They watched him walk awkwardly with his hostage down the corridor and out of the back door. In the car park, he thrust Louise to the ground where she retched and tried to catch her breath again. He dived into his blue car and, tyres screeching, hurtled away from the premises.

While Brett ran towards Louise to check that she was not seriously hurt, Greg swore and Clare told DCI Halford to put out an immediate call for Ian Law's car. "Get a helicopter up there! Follow but don't approach."

Brett squatted by the new recruit and asked, "Are you all right?"

"Yes," she gasped. "I'm sorry. I…"

"It wasn't your fault," Brett told her quickly as she got to her feet. "I'm sorry I put you in danger."

Louise held a hand to her bruised throat. "That's police work, isn't it? I just didn't expect my partner to … you know."

After talking into his phone for a while, Halford shrugged weakly. "Sorry. The bird's miles down the M1, called to a problem at Junction 26."

Brett stood and sighed with frustration. "I'd better update the boss," he said. "He'll be … a bit unhappy. Greg, why don't you go and see if you can get the locals to let you into Law's locker? Let's take a look at his personal belongings while we're here."

As soon as Brett had broken the bad news to Big
John, Greg returned, saying urgently, "You'll
want to see this, Brett."

It was hard not to turn away in disgust. Inside the
locker, the trophies from Law's killing spree were
lovingly lined up: a set of false teeth, a bloodied
toupee, some spectacles, a pair of red gloves that
would fit very small hands, a silky blue headscarf.
The smaller mementoes were contained in glass
bottles like scientific specimens: a putrid scrap of
skin, nail clippings, a sad lock of hair, a tiny silver
crucifix, the severed finger. Two rows of souvenirs of
cruelty. All along, they'd been in a police station.
Clearly, Ian Law had a finely tuned sense of irony. No
doubt, storing them at work was his snub to the
organization that had blocked his career. He'd not

collected any commendations from the force so instead he had collected trophies from his victims. The locker also contained a false moustache that should have been comical but, among the gruesome keepsakes, was repulsive. Like a metal coffin, the whole cabinet was an affront to human life, to humanity itself.

Brett grimaced distastefully but did not touch anything. "OK if we bring in our forensic team?" he asked Halford quietly.

The local officer was equally mortified. Finally convinced by the undeniable evidence of madness and murder, he swallowed uneasily and answered, "I think you'd better."

It was two o'clock in the morning. The faintly flickering light of the aquarium diffused into Brett's living room. Unable to sleep, he sipped a drink and watched the illuminated fish. Constantly in motion but somehow calming. He also thought about Ian Law, the killer who had been keeping an eye on him. Perhaps Brett had been like a goldfish in a bowl within Ian Law's warped world. Perhaps he'd been under the Messenger's spotlight. Ian had fed him fruitless scraps of information and he had busied himself, scavenging the futile clues. Ian had watched him floundering, as he expressed it in his final message. At least Brett hoped that it was his final message.

The mystery had been dispelled. Ian Law was the

Messenger. What remained was a feeling of outrage. It was the outrage that kept Brett awake. Not just a multiple murderer but a police officer! And then there was the thought of imminent confrontation. For everyone's sake Brett needed to capture Ian Law at their next encounter. The prospect of failure was too awful to contemplate. The responsibility did not allow Brett to rest. He would have liked to deny that he felt intimidated by Ian Law but it would have been foolish to do so. In a brawl Ian was clearly superior. Brett had no idea how he would counter that threat. He would have to make it up as he went along. And he would hope that John, orchestrating events in the background like an overweight magician, could somehow give him the edge.

Jaded through lack of sleep, Brett tried to invigorate himself at daybreak with a run in the sharp morning air followed by a steaming hot shower. What restlessness had denied him, he would make up for with pure adrenalin.

The core of the team had assembled in the incident room for a briefing. Greg had just returned from a dawn raid on Ian Law's house. His team had not found the fugitive policeman at home, so he reported that the serial killer must still be on the road. Liz remained on-line, coordinating the search for Ian Law and his car, and monitoring incoming reports for any disturbances that might involve him. So far, there had been only one. Yesterday in Worksop, a policeman who had stopped his blue car had been felled with a single punch to the stomach. His internal injuries had kept him in hospital overnight.

John also involved the behavioural psychologist in the meeting. Once Salma had listened to the latest developments with a worried frown on her face, she delivered her own verdict. "This man, Ian Law, he's into fame, right? He'll go for something like a public showdown. He's got an inferiority complex. In particular, he'll try to prove he's better than you, Brett. That's what he's been doing all along really — showing his contempt for you and the police force. So, he'll come on to your patch, lure you to the same place and try to humiliate you. Perhaps in public, definitely in front of your boss. And he said he'd do it soon."

This time Brett was inclined to agree with the psychologist. Her prediction seemed to make perfect, hideous sense. "At least it means he'll stop his random killing," Brett proposed, trying to salvage something from the predicament. "He wants it to be just me and him. In particular, he won't have Clare around."

"That's because he thinks I might just be able to stand up to him," Clare interjected vehemently. She did not like the idea of her partner becoming a sacrifice to the Messenger. Her disquiet was reflected in her tone. "With the best will in the world, Brett, you haven't got a hope on your own." To John she said, "I don't think you should sanction Brett facing him alone. It stinks. And it's not fair. Ian Law's got an obvious advantage."

More calmly, John murmured, "Thanks for your opinion, Clare. But our choices may be limited. Obviously, we need to make sure that Law *thinks* he's facing Brett on his own. That's what it's got to look like or who knows what he'll do. There *are* some things we can have up our sleeves, though. Despite my reservations, I'll request marksmen," he said, "but I can't get them posted till we know where he decides to confront Brett. And we'll have backup out of sight. All I can say at the moment is that I'll protect you as much as I can, Brett."

"You can't do a lot," Brett declared as a matter of fact. "Remember, he's a cop. He'll know all our tricks. He'll be on the lookout for them."

"He'll welcome them," Salma ventured ominously. "He'll want you to fail, knowing that John's looking on behind the scenes. Nothing would please him more."

"Isn't there a case for arming Brett?" Greg put in.

Brett shuddered, recalling his last encounter with a gun. "I'd rather not," he said. "Law's going to pick a public place, we reckon. I don't want bullets flying with people about. Besides, he'll anticipate a firearm and pick a situation that won't allow me to use one, I should think."

"I agree," Salma advised. "Didn't you say he'd done some research on you, Brett?"

"That's what Louise said, yes."

"Then he'll select the place very carefully for his own advantage. Your options," she said to John, "may be even more limited than you think. I wouldn't be at all surprised if he goes for a human shield again."

"A hostage?" asked John.

Salma shrugged. "I wouldn't discount it."

"Great," John muttered scornfully.

Interrupting the proceedings, Liz announced, "I've got something. Not what you think, though. A body's turned up on a Norfolk beach. Seems that the locals think it's Ian Lowe, based on that media picture we put out."

"That's a pity," John said in sombre voice. "But it explains something. No wonder we couldn't find him. When he drowned his car, he must have drowned himself as well."

Salma put in, "From what you told me about him, you can blame his father for that. Too much paternal pressure and abuse."

Brett had a different and alarming idea. He had realized all along that Ian Lowe was unbalanced and insecure. Now it was plain that he was much more insecure than Brett had anticipated. Perhaps, in questioning him, Brett had inadvertently applied too much pressure. Perhaps, Brett speculated, Ian believed that he was under suspicion of his father's death. Maybe, if Ian *had* pushed his father down the stairs, Brett's questioning had pushed Ian himself over the edge. Brett tried to shelve these thoughts and concentrate on the task in hand but thoughts of his responsibility gripped and haunted him.

"It's sad, but right now we have other business to attend to," John announced. "Let's keep focused. Anything else on the Ian Law situation?"

"A crash course in karate for Brett?" Liz suggested with her customary misplaced humour.

"There's not much we can do till he comes out into the open," Greg observed. "Till he shows his hand. We just have to hope it's not another killing spree."

"Body armour," Clare suggested. "Kevlar will stop a bullet. It may not stop Brett getting winded but surely it'll stop a foot going through his ribs."

"Good point," Big John said, nodding. "Check it out, will you, Greg?"

An uncomfortable calm descended on the incident room. The end of the saga was tantalizingly close, they all knew, but it was well out of their reach until Ian Law surfaced again. Their role as detectives was over. There was nothing left to detect. Now they were merely hunters. Worryingly, before they concluded the affair, they all expected that Brett would become the hunted. And the animal that would prey on him was utterly deadly.

They did not have long to wait. At one-forty-five, the telephone rang. Liz answered it, listened to a question and, in the expectant silence of the incident room, asked, "Who is it?" She got the answer that everyone was anticipating, covered the mouthpiece with her hand and nodded, "It's him. Says he'll only speak to you, Brett."

John eavesdropped on another phone as Brett said tentatively, "Brett Lawless here."

"To save you tracing this call," Ian Law said, "I'll tell you now where I am. I'm in Kent. Does that ring a bell? I'm in this nice cottage. White weatherboards. Next to an orchard. Get the picture?"

"Mum and Dad!" Brett said. His heart pounded.

Ian laughed. "OK. I've got your attention. Come and get me. I'll be waiting."

Brett shouted into the telephone, "Don't you dare..." but his stunned cry was wasted. The phone had gone dead. He cursed and looked up to the ceiling. "My parents! Haven't they suffered enough?"

John said, "I'm sorry, Brett. He really *did* do his homework. We've got to get cracking." The Chief swung into action. He bellowed, "Someone get OS maps of Kent in here. Greg, get that body armour sorted out. We want it here in ten minutes. Get on the phone to Kent Constabulary, Clare. Get them to take up position outside Brett's parents' place but tell them we're taking over as soon as we can get there. Make sure they don't do anything rash on their own. And Liz, get us a lift to Kent – a helicopter, or a plane that'll put us down at Gatwick."

Trying to shake off the shock, Brett interjected, "Ramsgate would be better."

"Whatever's going," John concluded, "as long as it's fast. Right. While we're waiting for transport, show us where your folks are on the map, Brett. Let's keep a clear head, everyone, and go in with a workable plan." John glanced at Salma. "Any advice?" he prompted.

"Advice? No. But he's doing pretty much what I thought – gone for Brett's patch. Not the patch I expected, though. He's taken hostages but he won't make any demands. His only plan will be to humiliate Brett. He's got a huge grudge against the police force and he's transferred it all to one man – you, Brett. He's going to work out his frustration through you."

"Great!" John muttered.

They peered at the map and Brett familiarized John, Clare and Salma with the area. They were still contemplating the task ahead, formulating tactics, when John looked up and shouted, "Liz! What news on transport? Speed it up, will you?"

"Hot-air balloons are no problem but something faster's trickier. Looks like I'm getting the chopper. It's on other duties a few miles away but I've requisitioned it in your name. It's headed our way now."

"Good. Will it take me, Brett, Clare and Salma?"

For an instant, Liz was tempted to refer to the lift required to get John off the ground but even she realized that this was not the time for a gibe. She wanted to be in the same job tomorrow. "Four of you?" she said, playing it straight. "Yes."

"OK. Clear a flight with air traffic control. And tell Kent to have a couple of cars standing by to take us to the house."

"I'm already working on it," Liz replied efficiently.

24

The entire street had been sealed off by the Kent Constabulary. Clusters of police vehicles were parked at each end. The whole area was crawling with officers, some in uniform, most in plain clothes. The small group from South Yorkshire boosted the numbers further. Arriving on the scene, Big John shook hands with the local CID chief and introduced Brett. "The man in the hot seat," he commented.

"And I hand over the operation to you?" the Kent officer enquired.

John replied, "For my sins, yes." He nodded towards the Lawlesses' bungalow and muttered, "In there, it's our man. We know him best."

"OK," the detective responded, unable to keep an expression of relief from his face. "My troops'll be at your disposal for the duration. The two marksmen at the front and three concealed in the orchard behind will only respond to my command, though."

"Thanks. But he'll want them all shipped out pretty sharpish, I suspect. Anyway, let's get on with it. Establish contact." John wiped the perspiration from his face.

Salma suggested, "You should talk to him first, John. He'll want to know you're here and then he'll demand to speak to Brett again."

The Chief Superintendent from Kent Constabulary handed a mobile phone to Big John and said, "Good luck!"

The shrewd detective muttered, "I'll need it." He pressed the numbers that Brett dictated and waited for a response. Eventually, someone picked up the receiver but did not say anything so John barked, "This is Chief Superintendent Macfarlane."

"Yeah," Ian Law grunted. "I thought it might be. I've heard of you. Top dog. A good cop, they say. Well, I've got some instructions for you. You'll have marksmen posted by now. Send them away – and shift Detective Sergeant Tilley. I can see she's out there with you. I don't want her around. And you can forget stun grenades. Ship them out. The merest hint of one and I get angry. Right? Your other odds and sods can go as well, including the psychiatrist if you've brought one. I assume you have. I don't want any of them near here."

"Before I do anything, I need to speak to Mr or Mrs Lawless. I have to know that they're well."

"No. You'll take my word for it. I haven't harmed them – yet."

"I can't do that. For all I know, they may not be alive."

"You know what I've got in mind," Ian barked. "Lawless is going to come in. He'll confirm they're fighting fit. But before that, everyone'll have to be shifted. I only want you and Lawless out there in front of the house." He chuckled and then said, "It's good, giving orders instead of receiving them all the time. I could get used to it."

"I'm going to ring off, Ian," Big John said disdainfully. "I'll think about what you're asking and sort it out."

Ian Law replied tersely, "You do that."

John summarized the exchange for the benefit of the local chief, Brett and Salma. Unnecessarily, the profiler said, "He's eliminating all threats so he can go about his business uninhibited."

Glancing at Brett, John asked her, "Will he harm his hostages if we don't do what he says?"

"Almost certainly," Salma estimated. "They're not flesh and blood to him, they're pawns. Sorry, Brett, but… Anyway, he'd probably sacrifice one pawn and keep the other for use later."

Brett inhaled sharply but did not reply. He wanted to give his opinion but he restrained himself. He was too involved to make sensible decisions. All of his training required him to wait for the verdict of his dispassionate superior. He looked to John.

"OK. We'll agree to his terms," John dictated. "Withdraw your troops," he said to the Kent chief, "but keep them ready to move in again immediately on my signal. You stay with me, Brett. Everyone else to move out. Clare," John said to her quietly, "I need you to do a special job. You see, it strikes me there's something missing – his means of escape. How's he going to get away? Make sure you stay out of his sight but check it, will you? Go with the others but double back. Then have a discreet look around, especially out the back. See what you can find. You won't be able to report back to me – can't risk Law seeing me chatting on the phone, he might think I'm plotting and do something drastic – so use your initiative. I know you've got plenty. Now's the time to exploit it." He paused and then urged them all, "Right, that's it. Let's get cracking."

Before she left, Clare looked at her partner and said, "All the best, Brett. Be careful."

Brett nodded. He was tense and uncomfortable within the protective vest. He just wanted to get the confrontation over with.

Using the telephone, Big John informed Ian that he was getting what he wanted. "Look out and you can see. Everyone's decamping apart from me and Inspector Lawless."

"Yes, I'm watching. Good. Now, you stay out there as a witness. Send him in – that deputy of yours, *Inspector* Lawless," he pronounced mockingly. "Let's see if he can get me this time!"

"I can't do that yet," John claimed. "You see, you're obviously setting up some sort of showdown between you and Brett…"

"The law versus the lawless," Ian cackled. "Right's on my side."

"If you're absolutely determined to do it, it's got to be fair. I can't put Brett into it until you release his parents. There can't be fair play while you're holding them hostage. You can control Brett simply by threatening them. There's no glory in winning a rigged game like that."

"I'll do a deal. As soon as Lawless is in here, I'll set them free in a flash."

"How do I know that?"

"Because I've just told you. That's it. No more haggling."

John put his hand over the phone, updated Brett and prompted, "Well?"

Brett nodded. "It's probably the best we're going to get." He was willing to accept Ian Law's terms because he wanted to free his parents as quickly as possible.

Talking to the Messenger again, Big John enquired, "And what do you want with Brett? What are you setting up?"

Ian laughed. "It's not a game of Cluedo."

"What then?"

"That would be telling. But you'd think he'd get me this time, wouldn't you? He's already had one go and failed miserably. I'm giving him a second chance

– a last chance. He can't be any good if he lets me slip through his fingers again, can he? That would be a resignation issue, I think. Or a sacking. Now, get him in here before something happens to his mum or dad. The door's open. Tell him to close it once he's in."

"All right."

"You're on your own from now on," John said to Brett. "He wants you to shut the door behind you, so I can't get in unnoticed. I haven't the faintest idea what he's planning so I can't brief you. Just do what you can. And watch out – you know what he's like."

"Yeah, I know," Brett murmured as he walked towards the front door.

This time, he did not linger outside the cottage. Without hesitation, he stepped cautiously inside. Just like his last visit, he dreaded entering the bungalow but for different reasons. This time, his parents' lives hung in the balance. Brett could not afford the luxury of dawdling. He had to rescue them. The fact that they had rejected him all those years ago was not significant. They were his family.

In the hallway, Brett sniffed the air. There was a strong smell of petrol. His pulse accelerated. Gingerly, he slipped into the living room and immediately gasped. His mum and dad were sitting side by side on the floor with their backs uncomfortably against the radiator. They were linked by handcuffs that Ian Law had threaded behind the pipe that led to the radiator. They had tape over their mouths and panic in their eyes. Next to them, Ian Law squatted like a barbaric ringmaster presiding over some degrading circus act. Obviously, when the intruder had invaded their home, they'd not had an opportunity to use the would-be weapon that they kept in the top drawer. Anyway, it would have been useless against a professional like the Messenger. With barely a glance at his adversary, Brett asked his parents, "Are you all right?"

They nodded.

Brett stared at Ian and said, "I'm here now. Let them go. You said you'd trade them for me."

"You weren't paying close enough attention to what your boss said. Not good for a police officer. I told him I'd set them free – in a flash," he pronounced mysteriously. "That's all. Now," Ian hissed, "I want to know if you're armed. Because, if you are, by the time you shoot, I'll make sure one of these two'll be in front of me. Your mother, I should think."

Brett spread his arms. "No, I'm not carrying."

Standing up, Ian said, "I believe you. You don't want to put your parents in danger." He laughed and declared, "I feel you're a man I can trust, so I've put myself at your disposal. You've got me cornered. Your chief expects you to bring me in. Any halfway decent copper would. And I took the liberty of informing the media that you've captured me. I told them you had me once before as well. If you let me off the hook again, they'll be baying for your blood, I should think."

"You're trying to ruin my career," Brett surmised.

"Yes, just like mine," he snarled. Moving away from Brett's parents, he began to prowl round the room. "Wouldn't you agree that if I get out of here, I must be better than you?" He glared at Brett through frenzied eyes.

Brett backed off, edging towards his mum and dad. He wanted to position himself protectively between them and Ian. "Quite possibly, yes," he admitted, trying not to antagonize the murderer.

"I'd be better than all those outside as well. I'll have taken on the best and won, all on my own. That's what I'll do. You see, I've got my plans to think of. I've got to kill thirteen more people yet. Unlucky for you. Then I'll have my name right across the country."

As calmly as he could, Brett nodded towards his trussed parents and said, "That's got nothing to do with them. It's just between you and me."

"You want this?" Ian teased like a naughty child, dangling a small key between his right thumb and forefinger. "The key to the handcuffs."

"Yes."

Ian halted by the fireplace. He spat into the flames and his saliva slapped against a log and hissed. "Nothing like a real fire," he muttered evilly. At the centre of the mantelpiece the old portrait of a little girl on her sixth birthday was proudly displayed. Ian picked up the framed photograph and peered at it. "Nice," he pronounced cynically. "Sweet. I wonder who she is?"

Behind him, Brett heard a strangled cry from his mother's throat.

"Is it precious to you, then?" Ian taunted them.

Brett wanted to bark, "Get your filthy hands off her!" But he restrained himself. He had to keep calm, and he couldn't afford to make matters worse by enraging the demented policeman.

Delighted to be able to destroy something of value to Brett's family, Ian bent down and offered the photograph to the flames like a piece of bread to a hungry bird. The flames leapt at the chance and began to devour the cardboard surround.

Brett tried to ignore the tortured, stifled cries from behind him and his own anger. Still trying to stay cool, he kept his eye on Ian. He was hoping for an opportunity.

Law continued to circle the lounge, carrying the key in one hand and the burning photograph in the other. At the door, he held up the key and yelled, "Come and take it from me, then. But I warn you, if I drop this photo, the whole place will go up. You see, I've already soaked the door frame and carpet around here with petrol."

Even wearing protective gear, Brett knew that he couldn't hope to tackle the expert fighter and win. Besides, he believed that Ian wanted an excuse to drop the makeshift lighted taper. A rash attack would provide him with that justification. But what would he do if Brett declined to react? The serial killer would not just walk away, because he knew that Brett could leave his parents safely where they were and follow. He'd summon a police team to overpower the Messenger, and then return to release his parents. Brett anticipated that Ian would not allow him to get the upper hand by refusing to fight. Abruptly, he realized that Ian was going to set fire to the room anyway. And he'd start it at the door so that Brett and his parents could not escape. They'd be trapped. That way, Brett wouldn't take up the pursuit. He would never abandon his mum and dad in a burning room. He would have to watch the killer escape again.

Ian snorted, "I'll let the flames set all three of you free. In a flash!" His gleeful, unhinged laugh was like a predatory animal's cry of triumph over freshly killed prey.

The sound of Law's squawking made Brett lose control at last and he burst into motion. He flew towards the madman in the doorway but Ian was far too quick for him. Ian's foot crashing into his chest felt like a cannon ball. The pressure on his sternum was extraordinary. It knocked every bit of wind out of him and he fell backwards, believing that his ribcage had collapsed.

Ian dropped the embers of Gemma's photograph on to the petrol-soaked carpet, waiting for a moment to make sure that the fire was taking hold and then scuttled to the back door. His manic cackling faded as he retreated.

Pain blazed in Brett's chest. As he gasped for air, he felt the noxious acidic fumes from the fire searing his lungs already. The polluted air ravaged inside his chest while the bruising from Ian's kick weakened him from the outside. For a while his body was incapacitated but his brain continued to function. He knew that, long before the fire consumed him and his parents, they would be overcome by the poisons liberated from the carpet and furniture by the flames. Heaving, he got up on his elbows. If he struggled to open a window, the fresh air that would allow them all to breathe more freely would fan the flames and accelerate the fire. Coughing, he began to crawl towards his parents but he stopped himself. He couldn't do anything for them while they remained manacled to the pipe. Brett groaned with pain and frustration.

Dark smoke had begun to spread across the ceiling. At least the floor was the safest place to be. Suddenly, Brett remembered something. As fast as he could, he dragged himself to the set of drawers. Using one arm to pull himself up while the other clutched at his chest in agony, he delved into the top drawer and clutched the spanner that his dad kept there. Keeping low, he crawled to his parents and the radiator. His eyes were beginning to smart in the corrosive atmosphere.

The door frame was burning and charring. The

carpet was barely alight but the fire had spread to the nearest armchair. Once an armchair was ablaze, Brett knew that there would be only a few minutes before flash-over – when the temperature would increase so much that the whole room would burst into flame spontaneously. The ferocity of the ignition would wipe out human life.

Brett's parents' grunting probably meant that he should leave them and save himself. Brett ignored their appeals. He fiddled with the adjustable spanner until it fitted firmly round the nut that held the pipe on to the radiator, then pulled on the handle but the nut refused to budge. Over the years the compression joint had sealed into place. Edging away so that he could apply his foot to the spanner, Brett took a deep breath of the foul air and kicked out viciously with the heel of his shoe. The spanner flew off but not before it had loosened the nut. Using his fingers, Brett turned the collar till it was completely loose and water was trickling out of the joint.

With one hand he grabbed the base of the radiator. With the other he gripped the pipe. Then he applied all of his strength to pull them apart. Suddenly, they gave way and water splashed all over him. "Water! Yes!" he exclaimed to himself. Using his thumb over the end of the flooding pipe, he directed the spring of water over his mum and dad, soaking their clothes and hair. When they were utterly sodden, he soaked himself again. Then he dragged himself and his gagged parents upright. Choking, he shouted, "Run through the flames and out the door! The water'll stop you catching fire. Quick, though! Try not to breathe in. The air's poisonous."

The air around their heads was thick with smoke and cyanide. "Go. Go!" he urged. He almost pushed them across the room. When they threatened to hesitate and lose their nerve at the sight of the flaming doorway, Brett cried, "Now! The room's going to blow any moment." He shoved them into the inferno and beyond. Dirty and wet, all three of them stood breathlessly in the hall. But they weren't safe yet. The fire was about to get out of control. Without looking back, Brett propelled them to the front door where John was hammering anxiously. Brett opened the door and delivered them into his Chief's hands.

Behind him, the draught from outside nourished the blaze. With a whoosh, the flames expanded furiously and the windows of the living room blew out in a fearsome explosion.

"Take care of them," Brett yelled to John. "I'm going after him. He went out the back."

"No!" his chief ordered. "It's too hot."

In the turmoil, Brett didn't respond. He turned back but straightaway he felt his face scorching and his eyebrows burning. John was right. He couldn't get beyond the living room door. Instead, Brett dashed past his mum and dad as John helped them away from the porch. Disregarding the ache in his chest, he gulped in the air and ran along the road and then down the entry into the orchard. It was a route he'd used countless times in his childhood. As he raced he even remembered taking the same path with Gemma. The sudden revelation hurt almost as much as his chest and lungs. His brain began to fill with long-lost memories.

The apple orchard was a series of long rows of skeletal trees. The green buds of this year's leaves were still a few weeks away. The lines of trees stretched from the string of bungalows down to the river. Really, no one was supposed to encroach on the orchard but the farmer was never harsh with the locals if he found them on his land. He allowed the children from the cottages to treat it as a playground as long as they didn't betray his trust by damaging the crop or stealing more than a little fruit. Now it was Clare's turn to wander in the maze of trees, not exactly lost but not exactly sure where she was. She knew only that the Lawlesses' cottage was somewhere on her left. In the deathly quiet, she could just hear the flow of the river to her right.

Between the apple trees there were straight and

narrow groves, forming an apparently endless network. It was in one of these natural alleys, near the river, that Clare discovered the motorbike. A getaway vehicle that could negotiate the confined and bumpy lanes. A getaway vehicle that certainly couldn't be followed by squad cars. Clare wished that she could tell John, but she couldn't. She wished that she had backup, but she didn't. She released the air from the bike's tyres and then settled herself behind one of the larger trees where she was likely to be out of sight of the rider. She waited and tried to compose herself. If Ian Law evaded Brett's clutches, she would have to tackle him alone in this bizarre arena.

Fifteen minutes later she heard the sound of his footfalls. He wasn't rushing but he wasn't loitering either. She peered out cautiously from behind the splintered trunk. Ian was approaching from the other side of the bike. She could not take him by surprise. He was wearing leathers and carrying a helmet in his right hand.

As soon as he stopped by the motorcycle, Clare came out from her hiding-place. Boldly, she stepped forward and declared, "Ian Law, I'm arresting you for the murder—"

"You!" Ian cried with contempt and arrogance. "Time to get you off my back." In a savage temper, he threw aside his helmet and launched himself at her.

Clare tried to relax, to remain self-possessed. She would not be able to match his power so she needed all the poise, precision and speed that she possessed. Probably more.

Brett ground to a halt. He was exhausted and sore. The pursuit seemed hopeless. The orchard was a large labyrinth and Ian could be anywhere. It always reminded Brett of an enormous web. Now, he wondered if Ian Law was the spider, lurking somewhere and sensing that a defenceless fly had strayed into his lair.

Suddenly he heard the sounds of combat and voices, the thwack of a fist on flesh and a shriek of pain. Frantically Brett spun round, trying to locate the fray. Deciding that the noises were coming from somewhere near the river, he sprinted towards it as fast as he could. While he ran, he tried to ignore the dreadful recollections of his childhood that crammed into his head and threatened to overwhelm and distract him. He heard a sharp intake of breath, a thud, a crack and another cry. Not far away. He carried on running towards the edge of the orchard.

There, where a row of bare trees ended on the river bank opposite the deserted golf course, Ian Law was clambering awkwardly on to a motorcycle. He seemed to have an injured hip and his left arm dangled ineffectually. He didn't bother with a helmet. He was leaning forward, turning the key in the ignition. The engine revved into ugly life. Brett forced his tired legs to accelerate. He wasn't going to make it. Ian was twisting the throttle. The motorbike roared.

Instead of speeding away, spitting mud behind him, Ian lost command of the bike. The wheels slid and he had to put his foot down to stop the machine toppling over. He grimaced with pain. As Brett neared him, he seemed to be peering at his tyres and mouthing oaths. On one side of his face there was a huge bruise. Amazingly, someone had stalled him by landing at least three heavy blows on him. It must have been a superhuman effort. When Ian looked up and saw Brett hurtling towards him, he attempted to take off again. This time, he kept control of the motorcycle by accelerating slowly. That gave Brett the time he needed. He could intercept the bike before it got up to speed. But he would not be able to stop Ian safely. It was going to be a risky undertaking. There would be only one opportunity. One perfectly judged flying tackle on a moving target. A high tackle that would get him sent off in a game of rugby.

Gasping for breath, Brett dodged between two trees and into the next grove, then he ran with all the speed that he could muster. Just as he cleared the last tree, the bike appeared in front of him. Brett flung himself forward, lunging at Ian's head and shoulders. He had to crash into him so that his full weight fell upon the fleeing rider's upper body. In mid-flight, Brett threw his arms round the killer's torso and barged Ian off the bike with his shoulder. The motorcycle carried on going for a few metres before slithering and collapsing on to its side. Brett and Ian landed in a heap but Ian struck the ground first.

With a horrifying crunch, his head slammed against a stone. Instantly, Ian Law was knocked unconscious. Two streaks of blood ran down his cheeks.

Unscathed, Brett dragged himself into a sitting position. First, he checked Ian's wrist for a pulse and found that it was still strong. The man was built like an ox. He would recover. In case he recovered too quickly, Brett handcuffed him. Then, to make sure he was immobilized, he used the belt from Ian's trousers to bind his legs to a sturdy, exposed root.

The motorbike's engine spluttered and died. Brett sighed and looked up at the sky. An ominous column of smoke rose over the trees and the distant siren of a fire engine sounded. Brett glanced around him.

It was then that he saw Clare. She was lying inert between two trees. "Oh, no!" Brett groaned. He staggered towards his partner and dropped to his knees beside her. Relieved, he saw that her chest was heaving slightly with her shallow breathing. He squeezed her shoulder and muttered. "Are you OK?" Getting no response, he brushed his hand against her pale cheek. Realizing how much he cared for her, he cried, "Clare? Clare!"

Her eyelids flickered. A long sorry moan came from deep within her. She muttered a curse and then asked, "Did I stop him?"

"Yes," Brett replied. "He's out cold. But are *you* OK?"

Her eyes opened. "Yes, just a bit faint. My wrist's broken and my leg..." Still slightly detached, she looked up at her partner and enquired, "What's that noise?"

"Fire engines. I'll explain later – when you're not so dazed."

"How about your folks?"

"They'll get over it."

"And you?"

Brett nodded. "I'm fine," he said with a concerned expression. He thought that it might be best to keep her conscious by talking to her so he said, "You know, Clare, there's something good to come out of all this. I learned quite a bit about myself. All those years ago, I never meant to hurt Gemma. She was on her bike. It was a bit too big for her really. She was out of control, heading for the river. I tried to stop her before she got into trouble but only made it worse by knocking her off altogether. That's what happened. If I hadn't intervened, perhaps she'd have just fallen off, or got a bit wet. I *was* responsible for killing her but it was only an accident – a terrible accident. But at that age I blamed myself. I tried to cover up, to deny what I'd done. That probably made me seem even more guilty. I felt so ashamed about killing my sister that I buried the memory – till now."

Through her agony, Clare managed to smile at her partner. She laid her undamaged hand on his arm and whispered, "I knew it. You were never evil." Then she passed out.

The star of the show sat in a chair, her bandaged leg propped up on a stool, her crutches leaning against a filing cabinet, and her arm resting on the table. Wheezing, John straightened up and passed the felt-tip to Liz. Clare looked at the plaster on her arm and the bruised smile on her face widened. He had written, *Commendations have been given for less, John McF*. "Thanks, Boss," she said.

"Not boss any more," John replied. "Case over, I'm a mere visitor now." He looked at his watch and said, "But I can get in another pint before my driver arrives. Yours is a bit low as well. Since your colleagues – miserable lot – don't seem to be fetching and carrying for you, I'll get you a can."

"Stop fidgeting!" Liz complained to Clare. "I'm still trying to write." She was halfway through scribbling her message, *You should see the other guy*, on her friend's plaster.

The door of the incident room burst open and Brett breezed in. When the small cheer died down he panted, "Sorry. Just got back. Didn't want to miss all of the party."

"We saved you a lemonade," Greg announced. He threw a can to Brett.

Brett caught it and said, "Thanks." He took a welcome gulp and headed for Clare. The queue waiting to sign her plaster dispersed as if Brett had some sort of prior claim. He knelt down by her and asked, "Have they patched you up all right?"

"I'll be fine," she told him.

"If you need any help…"

"It's OK," Clare replied. "My mum's come over to fuss me to death. To be honest, I'd rather… But thanks, anyway. How is it with your mum and dad?"

"Well…" Brett shook his head. "Not great. Mum's the problem. She'll pull through but it'll take time."

"And how about you?"

"Me? There's nothing wrong with me," Brett answered distractedly. "A bruise like a policeman's helmet on my chest, that's all. It only hurts when I breathe." He took another drink from the can.

"Really, I meant how are you with your parents?" she asked quietly.

"Ah," Brett murmured. "I guess that'll take time as well," he said solemnly. "There's no good fairy with a magic wand, I'm afraid, but ... I don't know... Things can only get better. We were on parallel roads, never meeting, but now I can see us coming together – eventually."

Clare smiled. She looked down at her fingers that protruded from the cast like worms from a hole. Without thinking, Brett had hooked his own fingertips under hers. She said, "Not much feeling in mine, Brett, and not much to get hold of."

Embarrassed, Brett let go. Then, theatrically, he looked round and said, "The Chief isn't here, is he? He didn't see, did he?"

Clare chuckled. "Right now, I don't care."

In truth, the party was muted. They had got their man but it was difficult to celebrate his arrest when the death toll was so high. None of the squad would ever really be free of the Messenger. In their heads, they would all carry different but equally horrifying images of Ian Law's deeds. In time, pushing the grim legacy to the back of their minds was the best they could hope for. On top of that, Ian Law had sullied all of them because he was one of their own. The whole of their profession had been tainted by one rogue. It was hardly a matter for rejoicing. And Brett's personal success was tarnished with guilt. While he was feeling better about his part in his sister's death, he blamed himself for Ian Lowe's suicide. He feared that he had hounded the vulnerable young man to the point where he took his own life. Ian Lowe was a martyr to the operation.

John drew Brett to one side and said, "I'm off any moment now. I just wanted to say thanks for your help. I look forward to seeing the papers eat their words about meagre probationers in the morning. That reminds me – in case I don't see you for a while, congratulations."

"What for?"

John grinned. "It won't be long before you finish your probation. You haven't left Keith any choice but to confirm your rank." He slapped Brett on the back.

Before he made his exit, John called for attention and then boomed, "It's been good to work with you all again. I can't say I enjoyed the case – I doubt if any of you would say that – but you got the job done. Think of it like this. There's thirteen people out there alive because of your good work. When people criticize us for not getting him quickly enough – and they will, no doubt – you think of those thirteen."

And John manoeuvred his hefty frame through the door, leaving a huge hole in the party.